DEDICATION

To the angels that catch me each time I fall.

R&R
A Feast of Words

By Maria Giuseppa

Dear Raffi,

Each I time I put pen to paper and spell out your name, I marvel at this correspondence of over forty years. We live in a world where air travel is easily accessible. We live in a time when we could watch each other on a screen while talking to our hearts' content. Yet, we have chosen not to see each other, not in person, not on a screen. We continue with our old-fashioned approach, prompted, I think, by the fear of losing something precious. Perhaps, we are only stubborn, set in our ways, too old to change.

Recently, change suddenly and unexpectedly surprised us.

Shortly after posting my latest correspondence, I realized that after the hundreds of letters that have traveled between us, I had signed my last letter "with love." Realized, yes, but only in afterthought, too late to retrieve it from the mailbox (and I tried). I have no idea what led me to write it now, after loving you all this time. But you, of course, understood and put it all in perspective in your response. This is the reason we are so good together. When one of us stumbles, the other always breaks the fall.

How comforting that you signed your response in the same way. Now that we are both "the surviving spouse," we can once again, without explanation, freely love each other as the good friends we are. Why is it so terribly difficult for others to understand that such a relationship can exist between a man and a woman, a relationship with no eroticism and no strings attached? At least no more strings than any other friendship attaches. Remember the strong feelings Isabel kept espousing on this very topic?

We knew each other before we met either of our spouses, or should I say *any* of our spouses? In either case, we knew each other better in some regards. We have certainly endured longer.

Do you think we have endured longer precisely *because* we kept that distance? No doubt that is a factor. Perhaps, it is because we write only what we want each other to know. We purposely leave out the messy parts. We take the time to rearrange the words, to develop the appropriate tone. Is this a fantasy life we lead? Real life does not often permit redos, erasures, and corrections.

On the other hand, we take the time to go deep. We think everything through and express ourselves more clearly. We trust that we can speak the truth without reservation or repercussion. In that sense, we have been more honest with each other than with any other significant person in our lives. We did, after all, speak that way when we originally were face to face, two young university students such a long time ago. We thought we were so smart, such intellectuals, solving the world's ill-begotten problems.

The world was easy to dissect. It was our own personal dilemmas that overwhelmed us. What drama!

Do you remember the arguments I had at home with my parents? I had to commute to school rather than live in a dorm. I had to work part time. I had to maintain high grades to keep my scholarship. And still they insisted on a curfew whenever I finally had a chance to go out. Back then I couldn't understand it, or stand it at all for that matter. Seems so trivial now. You, on the other hand, never struggled. You had all the time in the world and were my constant temptation to cut class or to skip work. But, oh, what great times we had playing hooky!

Enough of the nostalgia. Shall we move on to current events? Are you sheltering in place with a mask on? Are you sticking to bourbon as your medicine of choice? Are you spending your time watching television, reading books, knitting and crocheting perhaps?

I shall be waiting with baited breath for you to share some interesting tidbits.

Until then, I send my love.
Rachele

DEAR RACHI,

I color this letter with the yellow and orange of a noonday sun that reflects the glow of melting ice patches twinkling like diamonds on a frozen lake.

How on earth did we get stuck with these names? I know you hated it, but I like that your father called you Rachelina. When I called you Rachi, everyone thought I was speaking about some tough guy named Rocky. And then there was me, Raffaele. The only name I disliked more was its Anglicization to Ralph. I was thrilled when friends started calling me Rafe, and then you started calling me Raffi. Names are important. That is the first thing prospective parents should learn.

Yes, Rachi, you are the friend I love most. I remember quite well the strong opinions of your dear friend Isabel, but I have been thinking about what you said, that we only show each other a certain side of ourselves. On the other hand, after all these years, don't you think we have seen most of those sides? I must say most rather than all. I'm sure each of us has kept some secrets even from each other, out of embarrassment or in an attempt to avoid pain. Whatever the reason, there are probably one or two things we choose to keep forever to ourselves. However, neither of us could have been so adept at hiding over such a long period of time that we could have kept the essential part of ourselves from each other. I believe we know each other well enough for this not to be a fantasy at all.

In a way, it is more real than most other relationships. I say that because we have chosen to write rather than to talk, and we have put our innermost thoughts and feelings on paper. If the spoken word is indeed a powerful thing, in that once it leaves us it cannot be taken back, then how much more of consequence is a word put to paper? Not only is it permanently *out there*, it can be reviewed, revisited, even shared. It's too tangible to be a fantasy. Could be there was a need to sign your letter in the way you finally did. Perhaps it is something we both need.

By the way, you were not always the innocent one being tempted by this big bad wolf. I remember you initiating a few of our outings into the city or to the beach. That walk along the lake when the whole city was covered with ice was one of *your* brilliant ideas. If we hadn't held on to each other for dear life, we would have slid right into that lake, which, of course, was also solid ice that day.

When we didn't have the ice to contend with, those walks along the shoreline of Lake Michigan were most conducive to sharing our secrets. You see? Even back then we both had secrets. As you can see from the intro to this letter, the image of that frozen lake has taken permanent residence in my psyche. There must have been something beautiful about that day. Perhaps it was the laughter.

I seem to be falling prey to that same nostalgia you felt in your last letter. Who would ever have anticipated experiencing what we are going through now? Yet here we are. This period is so gloomy that returning to memories of happier times is about all we can safely do.

How am I handling this pandemic? Alone. Yes, as you mentioned, I am yet again alone. Tatianna broke things off at the beginning of this siege. After all, ours was not a relationship that could survive social distancing (or any other kind of distancing for that matter). To refresh your memory, Tatianna was known to you as the one who broke up my third marriage. Although, I did hear from wives numbers two and three recently, both doing well, merely assuring themselves that their financial security remains intact. They are, after all, accustomed to a certain lifestyle, as is my darling only daughter, Eva. Thank God she had the good sense to marry well and no longer needs her poor, old father's financial support. She does, however, still adore yours truly, and we speak at least once a week. Rachi, she is so beautiful, the very best I have done in life, right alongside my friendship with you, of course.

As you know, I live close to the Met. More than anything else, I miss my art. Sometimes, I ate lunch there for the sole purpose of prolonging my visit, especially on cold winter days, or rainy days, when I convinced myself those were my reasons for not leaving. And of course, there was no opera season, so there went my music. The one good thing about being alone is that I can at least listen to my music whenever I want, as loud as I want with no explanation or apology necessary. I have my piano still, but it has become a symbol of the passage of my youth. My wrists and hands no longer maintain the timing and the tempo that can satisfy the perfectionist you know me to be.

Speaking of perfection, I wish you could be here to cook for me. Even when we were young, if ever I stopped by to visit, I always left satisfied, filled with new tastes and aromas, meals of earthy simplicity that went so well with the ever-present Mateus. (Ha, what wine connoisseurs we were back then!) Now we are merely snobs. But what I would give for an evening enjoying your cooking, a bottle or two of that rosé, and conversation that lasts all night. There are times I regret letting all those other people in.

Ah, the things we cannot change. Be safe.

All my love,
Raffi

DEAR RAFFI,

First, I must say that the way you begin some of your letters ensures that they are more than words on paper. They are paintings you hang in my mind. Now I understand just how much you miss the Met.

Let us agree that poor Tatianna was not known to me as the one who broke up your third marriage. That distinction, as you know, goes to the same unscrupulous man who ruined marriages numbers one and two, and who, for the purpose of this conversation, shall remain nameless. I rather liked wife number three better than the others, perhaps because I knew her on paper only and for such a short time. As for Eva, you are right. She is the best of you, except the beauty part, which she got from her mother, number two, I believe. You always did like to surround yourself with beauty.

Perhaps that is, once again, the artist in you.

Although I met your first two wives in person, I never really got to know either of them. Matt and I joined you and Gwen for dinner whenever we were in New York. But as often happens with old friends, the three of us spent the evening reliving old times while poor Gwen sat on the sidelines. As far as Franny goes, I believe I only ever met her at the wedding, but I remember her being quite stunning. Fortunately, you always enclosed a picture of Eva in your Christmas cards, so I have in that way watched her grow into the beautiful woman she is now. She bears a striking resemblance to her mother as I remember her, while smiling your smile with her eyes.

Interesting that you should mention keeping secrets. Was that something that may have factored into your past marriages? Now you have me wondering about the parts of you I don't yet know. As for me, I'm a firm believer in the axiom that some secrets are better kept that way.

I know this pandemic has plenty of negatives, but it has given a steady flow to our letters. There were so many times in our lives when years went by without any contact whatsoever save the perfunctory Christmas card and exchanging of gifts via good old FedEx. Yet here we are again, right back to the way we always are with each other.

I certainly understand your missing the art and the music. For me, music is the worst. Although I can listen to it any time in my own home, I miss the grandeur of the opera house, the collective response of an audience, the applause and curtain calls. Not just opera, mind you, but all the other concerts I have missed. And theater. Please don't get me started on live theater. By the time this is all over, we will have missed an entire year. And still, we will be the lucky ones.

I am saddened that you can no longer play the piano as well as you used to. However, I have heard you play often enough to know that at your worst, you could best most other musicians. Please don't allow that cursed type-A personality that goads us to perfection in all areas keep you from enjoying the things you love. Take it from one who unfortunately is victim of that same curse.

Thank God that need for perfection never interfered with my intrepid attempts at new concoctions in the kitchen. I still love to cook. The satisfaction of creating a new dish was always worth the possibility of failure. Did you not know that you were often my guinea pig, so to speak? I loved, and still love, trying new things, and quite often experimented at those late-night sessions that turned into early morning breakfasts. I believe we drank Mateus for both of those meals if I am remembering correctly.

Believe it or not, I had almost a full bottle of Mateus the night before I delivered my first child. (That was before all the warning labels.) But every time she got into trouble as an adolescent, I wondered if it was my fault.

I heard that rosé is fashionable again. Perhaps you can remain a snob and still enjoy a glass for old time's sake.

You know, you are the only one that has ever called me Rachi. My husband had many pet names for me but judiciously stayed away from that one. It is quite surprising that he was never jealous, considering what a flirt you were back then. I notice you haven't changed much in that regard with your wishful thinking about not letting other people in. In a way you are right. They were always the strangers, at first befriending the *team* of us before going beyond to the *each* of us.

When we met on that first day of university, right from the very beginning of our friendship, we seemed to fit like pieces of a puzzle that neither of us had to force into place. Thank goodness for that. We were both so lost and confused those first few days. But once we found our rhythm, if we weren't in class together, one of us would be waiting outside the door of the other's classroom or lecture hall. We ate our meals together, usually on those crowded tables in the student lounge. At least that's where we ate the ones I brought from home. I was teased mercilessly for eating meatball sandwiches or zucchini omelets. (Italian food did not bask in the popular glow it has today.) Even if I could have afforded buying lunch every day, I would still have brought it from home most of the time. Since we usually shared, you surely remember that the joke was on the rest of them. My lunches were damn tasty. We both belonged to the Spanish Club moderated by that dapper professor from Argentina. He was such a character with his little mustache and insistence on playing tango music in class during our tests. Remember studying at adjacent study carrels in the library together? We were forever being shushed by one of the librarians. We spent so much time together anyone else we met along the way seldom got a one-on-one with either of us. It's a wonder that other relationships actually had a chance to develop. It must have been hard for Matt or any of the girls you dated to get their message across. Somehow, they managed. I guess even in a group, you can't hide certain feelings. Things fell into place for Matt and me when we realized we didn't live far from each other and could drive in to school together some days. Once you or I noticed that "something more" was going on, we were always happy for each other. We never let those new feelings for someone else compete with the ones we shared. Our relationship didn't have bells and whistles, but it was comfortable and secure. Our friendship was unconditional, so adding other people to our group of two was never a problem.

In a strange way, I think our relationship helped my marriage. I never stayed married out of desperation, nor out of fear of being alone or rejected. I knew I would never be alone, that I would always have somewhere to go, someone to turn to. This odd security could easily have become a negative. It could have kept me from standing my ground and working on my marriage, especially during a few difficult periods. Instead, it was a constant strength, always there standing in the shadows. It gave me confidence and a greater sense of self-worth. I knew that no matter what, I would always be important to someone.

I wish I could have returned the favor. I know you interject humor into the failed relationships of your life, but I cannot believe the breakups were not to some degree painful. Why is it that you always need to move on in your love life? You never once strayed from our friendship. That is one secret that I do know about you. You can be and, in fact, are a man of substance and constancy.

Let's pretend this is one of those all-night marathon conversations.

I'll go make breakfast.

Love you,
Rachi

10

My Dear Rachi,

I paint this letter in shades of gray with big, sloppy clouds leaking rain in the shape of tears.

Eggs over easy with a little toast and jam, and I am a happy man. Add the aroma of good, strong coffee, and I might swoon. (Do you still have your stovetop moka? I have one in every size.) Just to be clear, though, I never flirt with you—others yes, but never you. I am either completely serious about what I say or am mercilessly teasing. I leave it to you to distinguish which I am doing at any given time.

Next, your darling husband was never jealous because he had no reason to be. From the moment you first saw him, he was your world. And if I could see that, he would have been a fool to have missed it. Yes, he could be a royal pain on occasion, but he was nobody's fool. If I had to guess, I would say you probably were never even tempted. That's why we work so well together—yin and yang. I am always tempted.

Which brings me to my favorite topic: yours truly! Needing to move on, for your information, is not a character flaw of my own choosing. Are you sitting down? I will tell you something hardly anyone else knows. Wife number one left me, not the other way around. She was in love with someone else for quite some time before I found out. That is not exactly accurate. I did not find out; I was informed, by her and him together. I had no clue. I was completely blindsided by their ever-so-civilized announcement. I never realized how much more she wanted. Not more from life, not more from me, just more.

Insatiability was her predominant character trait, whether in material things or in people. As soon as she possessed what she thought was the *whole* of something, she needed to move past it, always in the hope of gaining more, bigger, better. Then, once she possessed it or them, they could no longer hold her interest. She completely redid our first home, and then immediately decided we should move. Having me as her husband was only the beginning. She needed every part of me, which I was only too happy to give. Once she decided I had given her all I had, she realized it was not enough.

I have seen her perhaps two or three times since our separation. She lives in a social stratosphere so far beyond mine that we only meet by chance. I have erased the entire five years of our marriage from my memory as if they had never existed. The only thing that remains is the feeling at the end, the shock of it, the disillusion.

Not to worry, no need to cry for me, Rachi. I was young. I moved on. By the time wife number two came along, I made sure I, too, was more.

As I think about it now, except at the very beginning, I never saw you in your married environment either. Did you ever outgrow your minimalist approach to life and begin to spend your time accumulating "stuff"? Was your home a grand estate that you passed on to the next generation? Clothes, jewelry, cars? Have you a treasure trove stored away somewhere safe? Are your blue-collar roots still showing or have you peroxided the hell out of them? I never once saw you in the state of "longing." You seemed always so content. Are you still that way now?

I have probably depressed you with my sad tale and annoyed you with my questions. Let's move on to something more fun. I have been preparing for the end of Covid. Here I am, in New York of all places, and in the restaurant business of all professions. On the surface those seem like the worst places to be. No, I am not trying to depress you more. Just listen. If so many restaurants have closed or are closing, that means that when this is all over, restaurants will have to reopen. They will have new owners, new concepts, or be in need of remodels. Think how much designing I will be able to do. So, I am getting a head start, putting some fresh ideas on paper. I am already in discussion with some of the more far-sighted investors. It is invigorating to have the creative juices flowing again. All we have to do is survive the pandemic.

And on that happy note, I leave you until next time.

Love always,
Raffaele

12

DEAR RAFFI,

Now I understand why we saw so little of each other during your first marriage. I remember Matt's concern about you being so out of touch that even your phone calls became short and infrequent. I chalked it up to your being busy building your business and clientele. Looks like we have kept some things hidden after all. I wish you had told me at the time. I could, at the very least, have shored up your ego a little. By the time you were married five years you were already very successful. I remember how proud you were of all that you had accomplished in such a short time. To see yourself through the eyes of someone who saw you as so much less must have taken your breath away. I could have been there with a little CPR.

Since we are being honest, if I had been allowed to make that save, you would have had the opportunity to repay it many times over. You are right to say my husband was nobody's fool, but there were times that I was. I allowed so much to go on around me unchallenged. It was not about a physical unfaithfulness to me, which in a way, is easier to forgive. No, it was more about an unfaithfulness to the equality of our marriage partnership. It was about keeping me in the dark about things, assuming I would not be able to "handle" them. It was about not acknowledging my role in his success because he never saw it. It was about making all the big decisions, and then surprising me with them, as if he were constantly giving me presents, but always of his own choosing, his own taste.

Every so often, I took inventory, counting which parts of me still remained and which had been absorbed by his stronger personality. There was no question that we loved each other, but there were times we were not good for each other. Still, we survived more than forty years of marriage. We raised wonderful children and were happy most of the time.

I hope he can see me now from wherever he is and know that those other parts of me are making a comeback. I am not as fragile as he believed, and I can think quite well for myself.

You ask me questions about my home, and I am surprised that I never spoke of all the changes. Looking back, I see large gaps in our correspondence. We always picked up exactly where we had left off, but sometimes entire years had passed with nothing more than a scribbled note in our Christmas cards.

I had always assumed that our home would be passed down to our children, and that I might even live there with them. Instead, as you can tell from my change in address, that's not what happened. I sold our rather large and stately house when I moved into this condo closer to the town center than our "country" home. When I was widowed, most of my decisions were dictated by financial necessity and practicality. I wanted no responsibilities such as mowing grass and shoveling snow and was happy to pay for the luxury. However, financially I would have been unable to keep doing that over an extended period. The children had already settled into their own lives within nearby communities. No one was interested in relocating their families and moving back home, so to speak. I did not want to burden anyone with helping me to care for a place that was much more than I could handle on my own.

Fortunately, the condo does have extra guest bedrooms and an area large enough to host family dinners. Of course, I updated the kitchen where I spend a considerable amount of time. In every other way, it is compact and comfortable. I still have a car, but I can walk to most places that I frequent. Although, I'm not doing much frequenting of anything during this pandemic. I don't even have to leave the building to mail these letters!

While I did let go of the house, I did hold on to some things. I brought with me my favorite pieces of furniture, very traditional, some fine antiques. I picked up a few pieces of art over the years that have special significance to me. Some, by local artists, were picked up at art fairs. Others are prints from the Art Institute here in Chicago. And my books. I kept all my books. Hundreds of them. There are bookcases in every room of the condo, and I love it.

I regret not keeping in touch during that time. It was a difficult period for me, perhaps too difficult to share even with you. In a way, it was a good thing that you were out of the country when Matt died and I was only able to leave a message for you at your office. Your presence would have brought back so many memories I might very well have drowned in them. Instead, I threw myself into practical endeavors and saved my grief for later when I could deal with it a little at a time.

You thought you were depressing me with your last letter. Look what I have just done. Your tearful clouds must have leaked a little on me, too.

Sorry. I will move on to lighter topics just as you did.

I am happy to sense your enthusiasm for the future. Tell me about some of your restaurant designs and ideas. As an avid foodie, I would love to hear about them. I know you have done some here in the Chicago area, but I wonder if I'll ever see them now. It occurs to me that you may have been here when those were put together, and yet you neglected to stop by to see us.

Curiouser and curiouser…

All my love,
Rachi

My Dear, Dear Rachi,

I paint this letter in the abstract. A canvas full of hands, fingers interlaced, male and female, young and old, morphing into wings and flying away.

Who would have guessed that we would be baring our souls at this point in our lives? This pandemic is such a constant reminder of our mortality that it prompts us to delve deeper.

Even those who are the love of our lives sometimes get it wrong. The things you recount about Matt that hurt you are things I know about firsthand. I did the same thing. After all, he and I were such good friends, in part, because we had a lot in common. Even so, I will not attempt to guess at his motivation, but mine was not always honorable. Mostly, I didn't share what I didn't want any of my wives to know, not because they were weak, but because I was. There were things I was ashamed of, things that somehow did not work out because I made errors in judgment, decisions that may have, morally speaking, crossed the line just a tad. I am not attributing any of these same motives to your husband. I am merely trying to explain that it probably had more to do with him rather than with you. It's all past tense now, anyway, and neither he nor I can undo any of it.

That said, after reading your last letter, I wish I could redo those five years I was married to Gwen. I wish now that I had shared more of that time with you and Matt. I wanted so much for my marriage and family life to be calm and stable that I glossed over a lot of things that, in hindsight, were red flags waving right in front of me. You and Matt would probably have noticed and then hit me over the head with them. Somewhere deep inside, I think I knew that. Still, I wanted to avoid the humiliation of someone else knowing.

I am relieved to see you moving on. I was afraid that you would be too used to being part of a couple and would be lost without your other half. It sounds as though you are making some very wise decisions. I know, too, that whatever you are doing, it is with a heavy heart. I am truly sorry for that. I can only imagine how much you must miss him as well as your former surroundings. However, I do sense a contentment in your writing, and I know you will be just fine.

I was an absolute wreck when I found out about Matt's sudden death. At first, I was angry about having to miss the service and not being there for you. Later, I was relieved. Selfishly, I just didn't want to be strong, nor was I sure I could be.

More than the regret of not being present after his death, my worst sorrow came from acknowledging my absence during so much of Matt's life. Without question I would have entrusted my life to him. How could we have meant so much to each other and still have allowed such an abundance of time and distance to fill the spaces that should have been full of sharing? We always picked up exactly where we left off, yet we kept choosing to live separate lives.

I still carry that money clip Matt gave me for graduation. At first I thought it was egotistical that he had his initials engraved on it instead of mine, or just a silly joke. Later, I came to value it for precisely the fact that it had those initials. It became a sort of good luck charm, and I keep it in my pocket even now when there are no bills for it to hold as no one accepts cash any more. I even listen to his favorite Steely Dan once in a while, raise a glass to my dear friend, and let random memories roam my mind.

I did come to Chicago several times. Each was a fly-in and fly-out sort of trip, all business. But now, the more we say to each other, the more I wish to say, and I would not at all mind doing it in person some time. Figures, just when we can't do it, I want to do it. Or is it because we can't?

Did you ever go to one of those Brazilian steak houses called churrascarias? You know, the ones where each server has a different cut of meat, and they make the rounds to all the tables? Customers accept only what they wish and as much as they wish. The "gauchos" keep circling back to the table to offer refills upon request. Side dishes are placed on the table to share.

Well, my idea is to do tapas in a similar manner. Each night, the chef prepares a certain number of tapas based on what is seasonal and available. Servers float from table to table offering a platter of a certain dish. When that is consumed to their satisfaction, the customers accept the next and then the next. The tapas could be meat or vegetarian, and extend to soups and desserts. The menu would be fixed price, not including drinks. The house retains the flexibility to serve those dishes that can be done well yet economically. The customer has variety and quantity as well as a convivial, communal experience. Would you go to a place like that?

Let me know what you think. Oh, and share something with me. What do you do all day in your compact and comfortable condo while you are sheltering in place?

Ti mando un grandissimo abbraccio,
Raffi

Sweet Raffi,

First we are ending with love and now *the biggest of hugs*. Lovely. But unfortunately, that is one more thing we cannot do, just as seeing each other in person is. I'm afraid you are falling prey to the forbidden fruit theory. I truly hope that is not all this is about. I would love to see you, too. I think we have been afraid of letting each other see what we look like. No matter how kind these last forty years may have been, we are no longer young, slender, beautiful twenty-somethings. I keep thinking that if you see me now, expecting the young me, you might be quite disappointed.

Then I found a picture of you the other day. Writing about your trips to Chicago reminded me that I had saved it. It was in an old magazine and taken about twenty years ago. To my surprise and great relief, I can see that even back then you had already changed. I'm not sure why I am surprised except that in my mind, you have somehow managed to remain the same. Even through the obvious changes I see in the photo, I still catch a glimpse of that handsome younger you I used to know. The eyes didn't change, nor the smile. But seeing them alongside the things that do change somehow makes me feel better. My hair color has changed, by nature as well as by choice, and I have gained quite a bit of weight. Yet, I'm pretty sure you'll find the girl you used to know, too. And after we both stop laughing, we can share a cup of coffee and start talking, and talking, and talking.

I must have saved this picture for a reason. Even when I look at it now, there is something familiar about it. It was taken at the grand opening of Prost und Pumpernickel not far from downtown Chicago. Matt and I talked about going there for dinner but never quite made it. I wish we had known you were going to be there. We could have met you and helped to celebrate your success.

I love your restaurant idea. I would definitely go. I like that I could look forward to new dishes each visit. And since quantity is not a problem, I could pass on my least favorites and take more of the ones I like better.

I recommend two changes. I would make it Mediterranean small plates rather than only Spanish tapas. Then you could include Greek, Italian, French, Middle Eastern, and North African cuisines. More variety, more universal appeal. On the other hand, not everything should be a surprise. There should be some elements of the meal that remain constant, sort of "signature dishes" that regular or repeat customers can always count on. I do see it as a fun place, especially for groups small or large.

What do I do with my days, you ask? Like you, I have yet to retire from my profession. The process has simply changed, but there is a greater need now for what I do than ever before. If I were in this for the money, I would be thrilled to be a psychologist at this particular point in time. Unfortunately, there is not enough money in the world to make me wish for this "thing" that we are going through to continue. My sessions are via phone and video chats. And they almost always break my heart.

I used to deal with career issues or irritating marital problems. Now, the clients are older, in a world that is not merely unrecognizable but unaccommodating to the vicissitudes of age or illness. Young people think they are better, that they know more, simply because they are exposed to boundless information. They have no clue that all their information is worthless in the face of the knowledge that any one of these "poor, stupid, old people" retains in that fraction of their brain that is still functioning. The family unit is turned upside down. Lost in the upheaval is the basic respect that each person thought was a given at this particular point in his or her life. People begin to doubt their purpose as they lose their self-worth.

I have often been the subject of jokes within my family regarding my ignorance of technology. I do need their assistance in setting some things up. However, I have been fortunate enough to be able to adapt well to the use of technology in my profession and in my private life. I must say my grandchildren were a bit surprised when they received my first text. It was a good surprise. And, despite their teasing, I think it strokes their ego a little when they are explaining new features of some device to me.

I do, however, understand that this is all extremely overwhelming for some. It reminds me of my grandmother yelling at the top of her lungs each time she used a phone, believing her voice had to carry over the entire distance between herself and the person with whom she spoke. And let's face it, as children we laughed. And now it's our turn to be the yelling grandmother.

Add to all this the loneliness and desperation brought on by the terrible disease all around us, and you will begin to understand that my profession is in a boom period. I have retained only a handful of regular patients, so I do this part-time, several days a week. I haven't enough emotional energy to do any more. I know enough about mental health to place strong safeguards on my own.

When I am not working, I stay out of my head as much as possible. That's why I like cooking, reading, listening to music, and watching television—pure, mindless, escapist television.

And, of course, writing to you and reading your letters. They have become my human touch.

Un abbraccio right back at you, Raffi,
Rachi

DEAR RACHI,

I paint this letter as a melting magnifying glass à la Salvador Dalí.

After absorbing the lifetime of pain and suffering that your patients have so carelessly—yet purposefully—left behind in your heart, it surely must ache with every beat. If you absorb it as I imagine you do, it cannot "not" become a part of you. What do you do with all that pain?

I am reminded of alchemy and transforming common metals into gold. I see you transforming the pain into empathy, understanding, and compassion. Then gifting it back to your patient as something comforting and beautiful.

Yes, I like to surround myself with beauty, but you, my dear, are the true artist in our midst.

I totally understand the importance of mindless activities as you said in your letter. Television is a perfect example. There is one problem, though. When it is so lacking in appeal that it can't even hold my attention for a little while, I find my mind wandering to all sorts of other places, some of which I don't care to revisit. It's why I was watching the stupid program to begin with, and it even fails at that. The entire purpose of watching is thwarted when it is simply bad television.

It may sound funny, but good music does the same thing as bad television does. It pushes me back inward and leads me everywhere and anywhere, the places forgotten and those I wish I could stop remembering. This damn pandemic gives us all way too much time to think. It has gone on too long, and I am getting restless.

I do remember the restaurant opening in the photo you found. As I recall, it was an interesting evening with some ups as well as some downs. Perhaps it was best that you were not there. That was more than twenty years ago, and I have changed quite a bit more since then. Unlike you, I did not dye my hair; it turned on me all on its own. In the picture, my hair was still dark. Now it is mostly white with intermittent "streaks" of black strategically positioned here and there. Fortunately, it is still plentiful.

Apparently, we have the weight in common, which, in my case, is already evident in the picture. I fancied myself still quite dapper then. Please don't burst my bubble. In truth, I am still somewhat vain about my appearance, but less so than before. My mind is a much bigger priority. I will readily accept a deflation of my ego with regard to my body, if only I can hold on to my mind.

Speaking of which, I like the idea of expanding my concept to include the food of other countries. If we move on with the idea, we could collaborate on the menu. Wouldn't it be fun to work together? Remember how a group of us used to brainstorm all sorts of projects and business ideas in that ugly, orange-walled vending machine room in the main building at school? Those ideas were usually the foundation for the all-nighters the three of us shared afterward in the basement of your house. We strategized until we felt giddy. It wasn't only the creativity that propelled us, but the sheer joy of using our brains. None of us ever got into the drug scene, but we were high on those nights (even without the Mateus).

I am not intimidated by the advances in technology. In my field, we began to use sophisticated design programs quite some time ago. Moving from them to other technology was a natural progression, so I was never overwhelmed by it. I am, however, selective. I learn only the things that I choose, perhaps because they are practical, a few because they are fun. But I refuse to lower my eyes and keep them affixed to a screen when I can look up and see the real and beautiful world around me.

In telling me about your new residence, you mentioned decorating it with prints from the Chicago Art Institute. I also have decorated my bedrooms with prints of favorite artists. I particularly like the reprints of the relatively recent Gustav Klimt. I have *The Kiss* and *Portrait of*

Adele Bloch-Bauer I (you might know it as "The Lady in Gold") in one room, and *Apple Tree I* in another. Klimt is one artist I would have loved to meet. I find myself incorporating his works in my restaurants quite often. The mood they evoke is comforting while adding just the right amount of color. Technology may be able to recreate, but not to *imagine* that kind of beauty.

Just as texts cannot duplicate the pleasure of writing these letters.

Write soon.

Love,
Raffi

Dear Raffi,

You view me in such poetic terms. I assure you that on most days I feel anything but. I do hope that at least a touch of what you said is true, and that I do give something of value to my patients. In truth, they have always given value to me. I have learned so much from the glimpses they give into their inner workings.

Speaking of the inner psyche, a picture of you developed in my mind when I read your letter. I could almost see you pacing around your condo like a lion removed from the wild. I know your nervous energy, constant moving, perpetual thinking. You must feel absolutely trapped at times, dying to be free.

Please don't let this plague get to you. It will end and you will scurry about in your natural habitat of hurry and accomplishment. Apparently, we are close to a vaccine. Although it will take a while to accomplish its goal, we can begin to see an end in sight. We are so close. Please don't stop that brilliant mind of yours from moving into the future. It would be a true waste. Allow the beautiful Klimt prints you mentioned to help remind you of the possibilities and calm your spirit.

We spoke of the group of us in some of our previous letters. Whatever happened to that girl you were with back then? She was a part of our group for at least two years as I remember. She was very sweet and we spent so much time together, but I never heard any more about her after our wedding when you moved to New York. Is that when you broke up? I remember her fondly. Do you?

Working together would be a dream. I would be like an obsessed fan meeting her heroes. No offense, dear, but I don't mean you. I mean all the chefs and restauranteurs with whom you collaborate. I would be awestruck and probably would embarrass the heck out of you. But I would love every minute of it.

I have been reflecting lately on the irony of being stuck indoors, living a sedentary life, passing the days with no need to apply make-up or to dress up or to play the gracious hostess. I have never been so free of stress. As a matter of fact, I don't think I ever realized how stressful my life was until now, when it has all but disappeared from my life. I am referring, of course, to my life outside of my profession.

Let me be more specific. This is the first time I can remember that I have never had to answer to anyone. It's a freedom that almost makes me giddy. It also is introducing me to a person I never knew before. Do you think my persona has been a façade all these years? Did I create a purely public me while shielding the secret core of who I am? Strange thoughts to be entertaining at my age.

When I think of you, I think, "What you see is what you get." But that can't be the entire truth because you are revealing things now that I never knew. I have a feeling there is a story behind the "ups and downs" you mention that cannot be seen in that picture I saved. Perhaps, that's the reason I kept it all these years. No pressure, you can share whenever you're ready.

Who are you really, Raffi?

Dimmi,
Rachi

My Dear Girl,

Who am I really? I am a caged lion pacing, impatient to be free to read your next letter. It is not a bad assessment. While you seem to be reveling in your seclusion, I am being zapped of all my energy and enthusiasm for life. I often feel I am deluding myself into thinking that working on my designs will lift me off this barren ground and help me to soar one more time.

Because both she and her husband work from home now, Eva's schedule is much more chaotic than it used to be. Our phone conversations had a regularity to them that no longer exists. There is no defined beginning and end to their work days, which are interspersed with constant distractions from their son Samuel's presence in their "workspace."

I must do something to maintain my sanity. Thank God for these letters. They have become a life-line. At least they now arrive regularly, and I wait for them with eager anticipation. I look to them as my connection to the outside world even though you are inside your secluded space, rediscovering who you are and wondering where the real you has been all this time.

My dear friend, I hate to contradict you, but in my humble opinion, you have always been real and genuine. For fear of what they think, you may have allowed others to pull the reins on some of your actions, yet that never stopped you from thinking for yourself and expressing those thoughts without restraint or hesitation. I always knew exactly where I stood with you, and I also knew why. Don't sell your young self so short, my friend. One thing you were not then and are not now is a phony.

What you may be mistaking for a put-on, outward persona may be what I think of as "Rachi's wall." Yes, I named it back then; I saw it as long ago as when we first met. You were private and contained. You never let anyone totally in, until you fell in love. You opened that wall just enough to let Matt climb in and then cemented it right back up again before anyone else could sneak in with him.

I wanted with all my heart for you never to regret that opening. As young and inexperienced as I was, I knew what that choice cost you and understood that it was not really a choice at all. That was simply how you loved, either completely or not at all. Therefore, if that love was ever betrayed and you were ever hurt…

Well, I hope you never were.

I find it ironic that you thought I was the genuine one. I was not. That's what happened to that girl. Toni was her name. I never liked being alone. I always had someone like Toni hanging around. We did things together, had a good time, even liked each other, but then I always moved on. If you remember Toni, you surely also remember Karen, and Annie, and some others whose names escape me. We were young, and it was the 60s. We played it loose and easy. I was fine with that. They were, too.

The only reason you thought I was genuine is that I always was genuine with you. There may have been things I never told you, such as the story of the Prost und Pumpernickel, or what really happened in my first marriage, or my second one for that matter, or the other times I… Well, you get the picture. But whatever I did say was always true.

I know we are coming down the home stretch of this pandemic, but it will still be months before our lives go back to some sort of normalcy. On the one hand, I fear I can't wait that long. On the other hand, I know I have no choice. I'm going to start concentrating on Thanksgiving and which chef to contact for a delivered meal. Eva is too afraid to spend the holiday with me in case she might be a carrier. I am hoping I can at least have a traditional meal delivered. And I will absolutely be well-stocked with bourbon and vermouth, bitters, cherries and anything else I might need to keep my beloved Manhattans flowing. For sure, that's something to be thankful for.

How about you? Does anyone in your family feel safe enough to gather with those outside of their own household? You're probably planning the entire meal.

Even if it is just for one.

Losing my patience,
Raffi

Dear Raffi,

Something I will always remember from my high school days: JFK was shot, and subsequently, Oswald was murdered on national television right before our eyes.

It was right around Thanksgiving that year. I have always looked back on that day as the strangest Thanksgiving ever—until today.

For the first time in my life, I spent a major holiday without my family, without the cooking and preparation, without shopping and dishes, without stacks and stacks of dishes. Yes, I had a delicious dinner courtesy of my family who also provided a video get-together. We certainly all worked hard at making the best of a terrible situation.

Every year by the time everyone leaves, I am too tired to move. Now here I sit on Thanksgiving evening, sipping an excellent port, my feet up, and relaxing in front of a fire, writing to you once again.

Upon reflection (which I do quite a bit of lately), the most bizarre part of this day is not what you might think. What surprises me most is that *this* is the best part, that I look forward to sharing even a miserable day with you, my best friend.

How did you spend your day? Did you succeed in having that gourmet restaurant meal delivered? How many Manhattans did you consume before dinner? Did you spend some time, at least at a distance, with Eva?

I must admit that video conferencing technology has been a savior; however, I can't help feeling that I am on a home version of Hollywood Squares. I like seeing everyone, but I still feel somewhat removed, a feeling (I hate to admit) with which I am becoming quite comfortable. Sometimes being an integral part of other people's lives is overwhelming. Sometimes merely standing on the sidelines makes me feel much more at ease.

Listen to me getting all morose. I should instead, on this of all days, be listing all the things for which I am grateful. I am thankful to be alive, comfortable, loved. I am thankful that I have not gotten bitter and cynical. Given the chance, I will always choose to love, and I am grateful for that part of who I am. Another thing I will always choose is leftovers. I didn't have any this year, the most unforgiveable thing so far about this pandemic.

In gratitude,
Rachi

Dear Rachi,

I should paint this letter with a turkey, or a food-laden table, but I can't. Too sad. Even after two lonely Manhattans—too sad.

You know I was never very knowledgeable about sports, yet a sports analogy is what comes immediately to mind. When I think of you being on the sidelines, it reminds me of the coach on a football team. He may not be on the playing part of the field, but he is as integral to the game as any player. It is the way you have always been. Like the coach, you stand on the sidelines, you notice every detail of the game, you direct the plays and influence the outcome, but you never take the field. You never become one of the team. Part of you was always a loner. I will dare to speculate that it was probably so even in your marriage.

I say this without judgment and with more than a little admiration. This, I believe, is how you always manage to remain true to yourself. You created a picture of me recently as a caged animal, roaring to escape. I see you in a similar pose. In your case, however, the cage is in your mind. I remember that every time you needed to make a major decision in your life, you paced. It never mattered where you were physically; your mind kept you prisoner until you worked out a solution. I watched you wear out a path of grass in the park. I imagine you now rendering a carpet threadbare in your room. You pace, focused, oblivious to your surroundings, until you find your way out.

You never asked what I thought until after the fact, when my opinion would not be a consideration in your decision. I could have been insulted, even hurt. But you didn't consult anyone else, either. It wasn't because you didn't care about me or them. I know you did. But you left the impression that you never needed anyone else. No, you never were a team player. And then I introduced you to your husband and everything changed. You were happy to join that team of two.

Not sure exactly why I just went off on that tangent.

Yes, I did have a wonderful meal. I asked that they leave it traditional and not get carried away with all that avant-garde, tofu turkey stuff. What a shame you are not here. They brought enough to feed a family. Yes, I had leftovers, and I truly wish I could have shared them with you. I did think of you, however, and a toast to our friendship gave me a magnificent reason to have that second Manhattan.

I spoke to Eva on the phone. She spent the day with her husband and three-year-old Samuel. Thank God he is probably too young to understand what he is missing. But of course, his parents feel bad for him, and me, and themselves, and boo hoo hoo. They are asked to shelter in place on their comfortable sofas, in their comfortable homes. They are not being asked to go off to war and be wounded or killed in some strange place like every other generation has had to endure. We had Vietnam, remember?

I know. I am sounding old and cranky. I will end my letter as you ended yours, in thanksgiving. I am grateful for the life I've had, for the things I've seen and felt. I am thankful for the people I have known and loved.

Happy Thanksgiving,
Raffi

Dear Raffi,

The last paragraph of your last letter was entirely past tense. Please don't do that. I need you in the present and in my future.

You speak of "having loved" as if you are done with it. You will never be done with it. You will walk back to your museum one day and meet another Tatiana, and thereby spring suddenly back to life. She will hesitate. You will charm. She will smile. You will undress her with your eyes. She will invite you. You will accept. And before you realize it, you will be in present tense once more.

Forgive me if I misjudge you. Perhaps it is Samuel who will bring you to the present. Speaking of Samuel, how could you, for three years, neglect to inform me that you have a grandson? You could, at the very least, have shared his birth with me. What other major secrets are you keeping? Now, you have me wondering if perhaps I am not the only one who doesn't play well with others. At least send me a picture when you have a chance. (Speaking of pictures, I have not forgotten that you still owe me a story about your night in Chicago.)

Allow me to return to the point I was trying make. You might consider holding Samuel's hand and bringing him with you to your museum. You may begin to nurture the next generation of art lovers by showing them how to be open to the beauty that surrounds them.

Despite our bravado, I think we were both a little down on Thanksgiving. But cheer up! Christmas is coming.

When I gave up Easter dinner last spring, I did so anticipating that my family would be together for Christmas. Who would have thought things would be this bad for this long? So, I'm guessing Christmas will be pretty much like Thanksgiving. We will be eating alone. No grand fish dinner on Christmas Eve. No roast on Christmas Day. We need to find a way to make it a celebration somehow. I still intend to give out presents. I've ordered everything online and am in various stages of wrapping. Members of my family can, perhaps, exchange gifts through the door and at least see each other's face for a moment.

What if you found me on the other side of your door one evening, hand delivering your yearly bottle of bourbon? Would you invite me in to share it? Do you think we would finish it? I'll have to buy a better brand this year just in case.

Tell me about your plans for the holidays. Maybe I'll get some bright ideas.

Keep smiling,
Rachi

Dear Rachi,

My painting today is simply my own version of "la luna." Not the American moon countenance, but the Italian moon. La luna, white and glowing, peeking full-face through a floating cloud, wearing a pacific smile, eyes looking downward, absorbing the calming vision of Vesuvius and the Bay of Naples.

My last letter did catch me in a glum moment. Fear not, it has passed, in part, thanks to your letter, and *hence, the smiling moon!* I know this will eventually have to end. We may find ourselves in a "new normal," but almost anything will be better than this.

I never did well with small children. I don't know what to do with them when they are too young to understand much beyond a full stomach and a clean diaper. Perhaps that is the reason I have never mentioned Samuel before. I have always had a difficult time relating to little darlings like him, Eva when she was young, or nieces and nephews through my marriage to Franny. I feel uncomfortable with them. I don't know what to say to them or how to act with them. I have this feeling that they can see right through me and that they don't like what they see. I never even changed Eva's diaper. It is a good thing that whenever I see Samuel again, he will be beyond that stage. I do remember, however, when I first began to bring Eva with me to the museum and how enthralled she was. I'd be willing to bet that before Covid, she had already brought Samuel there many times. At least, I hope so. Right now, I don't care where we meet. It would be so good to see them both.

You asked about Christmas. Yes, it is gearing up to be a repeat of Thanksgiving. I remember stopping in at your parents' home for a few hours one Christmas Eve and getting a taste of your celebration. Several of your male relatives stood over the utility sink in the basement shucking clams and oysters by the dozen, consumed raw with a squeeze of lemon. Upstairs, there was a parade of women bringing an endless stream of platters from the kitchen into the dining room.   The stove was guarded by several other women, your grandmother stirring the tomato sauce filled with *calamari* while the water boiled for the spaghetti. Your mother was frying batches of the *"fritto misto,"* that salty, crunchy assortment of fried fish and vegetables—*calamari*, *baccala*, scallops, zucchini, and artichoke hearts the ones I remember best. I was surprised by the sound of a timer indicating the moment to plate the other fish that was baking in the oven, the whole red snapper that apparently was your mother's specialty. Of course, the cold dishes—green salads, *scungilli* salad, and broccoli with olive oil and lemon—were already on the table along with baskets of fresh bread.

After hours of non-stop talking, teasing, and laughing, everyone began to wander into the living room, which I had somehow missed seeing until then. There was another long table set up with every possible available space filled with a mind-blowing assortment of desserts. The children were already covered with the powdered sugar from the *pizzelle*. And just when I thought I could not eat another bite, I found myself "munching" on *panettone* and *torrone*, some biscotti, and even mini-cannoli. Then your Zia Luisa handed me a plate filled to the brim with fruit, nuts, and hot chestnuts, reprimanding me for not eating them before the desserts. And, oh, by the way, I had forgotten the lupini beans.

After all these years dealing with restaurants of every caliber, I can't imagine any of them outdoing the feast I found that night. Even in memory, I remain amazed at the sheer quantity and quality of fish that was being prepared, served, and eaten. And nothing will ever compare to the feeling. All those people reveling in that sense of family and companionship. I was not the only non-family guest. There were new boyfriends and girlfriends, neighbors, a new arrival from Italy, a co-worker here and there, not one of us made to feel uncomfortable or out of place. We were all enthralled by your great uncle Dominic's stories of his first Christmas here in "America" without family or friends and Zia Luisa's recollections of holidays spent while a world war ravaged their cities and farm fields. Your grandparents remembered days of empty stomachs and empty pockets, grateful that those days were a part of their past. Perhaps that is why no one was ever turned away. Anyone could have walked in that door and been welcomed and fed.

It was amazing.

My family was never like that. They were not unkind, merely "selective." They had to be. They knew that in our home the other shoe always dropped, a fact we preferred to share with the smallest of audiences.

Speaking of dropping things, it's strange that you should bring up the subject of my door and standing on the other side of it. I almost lost mine recently. There are so many deliveries coming into the building since Covid, and quite a bit of traffic floats past my door as my apartment is directly opposite the elevators. A rather large load cascaded off the delivery cart with a number of heavy packages crashing against my door. Saying that I almost lost my door was a bit of an overstatement, but it did suffer many bruises. It will need repair, and certainly a new paint job.

But banged up or not, you might have to revive me from an absolute fainting spell if ever I find you on the opposite side of it. After the smelling salts, I would be thrilled. Bourbon sounds good, but we probably wouldn't need it, we'd have so much to say. I would hug you and hold you for a long time, just to be sure you were real. Obviously, I am really missing human touch. I don't mean the Tatiana kind. I miss the kind that comes from the heart, from the memories, from the loneliness.

Yes, I will own it without shame or hesitation. I am lonely. I wish you were here. For the first time in my life, I am longing for something other than a lover. I want a true friend. You are the one.

Lovingly,
Raffi

DEAR RAFFI,

I have temporarily switched beverages and am sipping a gin and tonic. Don't ask why. Okay, I'll tell you. I like gin. I have plenty of it and I'm trying to use up what I have before I buy more. It is refreshing and reminds me of the summer I have missed. This is the part young people don't get. The time they are losing, they *can* make up. We older folks have lost almost a year that we will never get back. Our bodies did not stop aging. The travel we could have done this year we may be unable to handle next year. It's done. Some of our last chances could be gone. We all tried so hard to plan for our old age, but who would ever have anticipated this? How could we have prepared for this?

Guess we chalk one more thing up to "that's life" and move on. I am ready for Christmas. We are gathering here, one masked family unit at a time, at my door. We will exchange gifts, and then that unit will go back home and the next one will come. My daughter's family will come first and when they leave, my son's family will stop by. We will each open one gift together.

You rekindled so many memories for me of Christmases past. I was always happy on those festive occasions when you were able to join us. I regret that I am only now becoming aware of how much sorrow you held inside and that so many days were spent dealing with such an undercurrent of anxiety. The worst part, of course, is that you carried it alone.

This year more than ever, I am determined to make all the fish dishes and give them out as each family leaves. There is so much more packed into each of those dishes than the actual ingredients. Each one of them was favored and requested by someone in the family and kept as part of the meal to please them. It is still like that today. Someone insists on a particular dish; they like the taste, sure, but it also holds some holiday memory for them, perhaps a moment from their own childhood, or the memory of a loved one that is no longer here. In other words, each dish has a story, which in most cases has been told over and over. It is my desire, as it was my mother's before me, and her mother's before her, to remember it, to retell it through those preparations, to hold it dear, to watch the faces of everyone at that table as each of those memories is rekindled, all the while creating new ones for the next generation. To see the smiles, hear the sighs, notice the satisfied expressions as the meal continues—for the cook, that makes it all worth-while.

And so, we will have dinner and gifts as usual, only separate and apart, each in our own space. I will have to imagine the faces. We are doing our best to make a bad situation better. I *have* to cook the fish and share it. I need to do this for the sake of my sanity.

I have a small Christmas tree. I mean *very* small. How small is it? Small enough to fit on a table, a side table. I'm sure you remember that I am quite vertically challenged. I am convincing myself that this arrangement better fits my size.

The table is draped in gold lamé, and I have placed all the wrapped packages around the table on the floor. I think it looks pretty darn festive. Also, I am displaying an Italian Nativity scene and playing Christmas carols on my phone. Ho, ho, ho.

I think I need another gin and tonic.

I keep thinking about what you said about my family's Christmas Eve dinner. You are right. Anyone walking in that door would have been welcomed, not only on Christmas Eve, but any time. I tried to make my own home like that, as well. Matt was always on board. I have plenty of regrets about my life, but being welcoming and loving is not one of them. Neither of us ever gave it a second thought. If I have instilled anything in our children, I hope that is it.

I have finally made up my mind. When this whole thing is over, I am coming to New York. We will meet at the museum and go on from there. You will escort me to one of your most excellent restaurants, and we will cab it back to your place to sleep it off. Then we will have breakfast and an all-day talk fest until we are completely satiated and sleepy again. And when you awake the next morning, I will be gone. And we will both wonder if it ever really happened.

I hope your door will be ready by then.

Merry Christmas.

Love,
Rachi

DEAR RACHI,

Christmas was sad. Like Thanksgiving, I have no word for it, and definitely not a painting.

I spent time talking to Eva and am now up to date on all the "firsts" that I have missed with Samuel. Apparently, his vocabulary is quite amazing for a three-year-old, including some "adult" words that no one knew he had heard. His father's work-from-home routine often becomes rather frustrating, I hear. (So did Samuel.)

Eva is spending a lot of time reading to him, and he has already begun to pick up some words on his own. He also has discovered watercolors and has a particular fondness for frescos. Sounds like their place will need a bit of an overhaul after this is all over.

Speaking of overhauls, I am speaking to a painter I know about my door. I have so few outlets for my creativity lately that I am investing what is probably way too much time in a simple door. But it occurred to me to make a statement with it, letting it stand out in some way, perhaps a mural or fresco of my own. Hopefully, there is not some rule against that in the fine print of the *condo constitution*. We'll see. In the meantime, I'm open to bright ideas.

By the way, I received the bourbon on Christmas Eve and immediately put it to good use. Thank you for also including the cherries for my Manhattans. Incidentally, another first I missed was Samuel's unexpected encounter with maraschinos. His father, who was introduced to Manhattans by me shortly after he was introduced to Franny by Eva, unwittingly left his glass within Samuel's reach. And now we have a new member initiated into our Maraschino Society.

Unfortunately, it looks like even after this pandemic, I might be drinking at home. Several of my favorite places will not be reopening. You mentioned not factoring this pandemic in for our old age planning. Not having planned for this also holds true for businesses. How could businesses possibly have anticipated anything like this? Even if they have a reserve, no one has one large enough to last this long. This is the end of so many dreams. And this pandemic has yet to reach the finish line.

The vaccine news, at least, is promising. Between that and warmer weather, perhaps spring will see the beginning of some relief. I certainly hope so.

I like your idea to visit me and to stay a while. Tell me again why we have waited this long. More than a drinking partner or fellow conversationalist, we used to laugh together. I most of all miss the laughter.

Now, it's my turn to have an idea. Since we both have figured out texting, let's text each other at midnight on New Year's Eve. I know it's a step out of our comfort zone, but it may be the only thing that gets us through one more lonely holiday.

I look forward to exchanging well-wishes in a few days.

Love,
Raffi

Dear Raffi,

All that mentioning of Manhattans brought back a lot of scenes from our youth, the most prominent one being the day Matt and I got engaged. He had always been a wine sort of guy, with the occasional beer thrown in at summer picnics and boys' nights out. That night a group of us went to celebrate my saying "yes." You bought a round of Manhattans for everyone. Matt had always demurred when it came to hard liquor, but being easily swayed while in the celebratory spirit, he decided to try it. A surprise to even himself, he loved it. It was like a locked door had suddenly opened and let in a whole new world.

It became the first step to experiments with gin and vodka, ushering in a martini phase. That was followed shortly thereafter with rum and Cuba Libres. Then came the short-lived tequila stage, which brought him eventually back to bourbon and the clear favorite, the Manhattan.

I didn't always join him in drinking them, but I loved the maraschino cherry soaked in that combination of bourbon and vermouth. Matt liked them, too, so he began to add two of them to his drink. That way there was always an extra one to share with me no matter what I was drinking.

It's funny which little things you miss most when you lose someone. I never imagined it would be maraschino cherries. It's just that what happened with the drinks was merely the beginning. That eagerness to experience new things that started with a simple cocktail spread to other areas of his life as well. And he always took me with him. Once he was gone, that door closed behind him. Sometimes, I actually visualize a closed door for which I have no key.

Sorry, Raffi. It is a dull, dreary, wet-snow kind of day in Chicago.

Rachi

Carissima,

Being the brilliant architect that I am, I can assure you that a door, by its very nature, can swing both ways—and also, that it does not always need a key.

Love,
Raffi

Dear Brilliant Architect,

This time, I will paint a picture.

A man, very much like you, is standing in the middle of the canvas holding an upside-down umbrella. Rather than repelling, it is catching what is falling from the sky—not rain, not hail, not sleet—but a windstorm of maraschino cherries that fill the umbrella and all the ground around it.

The man is smiling.

His lips are the same color as the cherries.

Yours truly,
Rachi (who is asking you to resist any attempt at psychoanalyzing this)

My Dear,

Glad you're feeling better. It's almost a new year.

Love,
Raffi

P.S. Is this worth a stamp?

RACHI: Happy New Year, Raffi. *Cin cin!* All my love.

RAFFI: Happy New Year, Rachi. Hugs and kisses, hopefully real ones, very soon.

Dearest Raffi,

That was fun. It felt like we were together on New Year's Eve. I did not dress up. Did you? I did, however, have some bubbly. I prefer Asti rather than Champagne. I think that makes me what we used to call a "cheap date." You probably had the expensive stuff. Good for you. Under these strange circumstances, at the very least, we should each have what we want.

Here we sit, beginning another year. We all hoped that when last year ended, we could have locked it up and thrown away the key. Instead, ahead of us, there is more of the same. Except, I intend to shake things up a bit.

I have decided to take a "staycation." I contacted each of my patients and let them know I will be unavailable (except for emergencies) for the next two weeks. I have nothing in particular planned except a respite from all the emotional turmoil of their lives. I will remain as I am, alone in my condo. I merely need a break from others entering into my emotional space.

I need to do something creative that puts me "in the zone" and keeps me there until I feel refreshed and recharged. It will probably be cooking or baking although I don't want a surplus of anything that I will feel obligated to eat. Perhaps, I can find recipes for things that will freeze or otherwise keep for the next few months until I can share.

I hope you are right about spring. After being vaccinated, I think I will still be hesitant to fly. I have always enjoyed car trips. Driving out to some resort area not too far from the city sounds like heaven. Walking the semi-deserted shoreline of a nearby lake, greeting the random, masked stroller along the way, watching a sunrise or sunset… What do you think? Sounds good, doesn't it?

If you start receiving two or three letters a day, you'll know that my "staycation" has morphed into a "borecation." Wish me luck.

Love,
Rachi

RAFFI: Rachi, I know this text is totally out of the ordinary, but please check your email. It's urgent!

RACHI: Raffi, give me a few moments for the mail to load. The computer was turned off.

Dear Rachi,

I'm sorry but I couldn't wait for a letter to reach you. I am frantic. Eva has been hospitalized. I just received a call from her mother, also frantic. They are running more tests, but the doctors have already ascertained that Eva has Covid. The doctors tell us to be reassured since she is young and healthy. I am getting all the news second—and even third—hand. We are not permitted in the hospital.

I don't understand why, if she is young and healthy, a hospitalization is required. She must have a *very* bad case of it. I want to speak to a doctor directly, but they don't have the time to communicate with each family member. Both Eva's husband and Samuel have tested negative. The doctors speak to her husband, Michael, who then tells her mother, Franny, who relays it all to me. It is almost like a weird form of the telephone game only not at all funny.

You pictured me as a caged animal before. You should see me now. I do not do patience well.

Yes, Raffi, I am here and just read your email. I am so sorry to hear about Eva and wish there was something I could do to ease your worry.

Try to be the calm in the storm. Surely, Franny and Michael and Samuel are in just as bad or even worse shape than you. Be there for them. Ask them what they need, what you can do to help. It will offer relief for them and keep you from drowning in your own anxiety.

When you've had enough and find it necessary to blow off some steam, talk to me. Texting, emailing, calling, whatever means suits the moment. I will be here.

Please don't start thinking the worst. Even healthy people who contract this miserable illness may have difficulty breathing. Being in the hospital is where they can get a little oxygen. It may be as simple as that.

Prayers,
Rachi

RACHI,

I know more now. Eva waited too long before going to the ER. By the time she got there by ambulance, her lungs were badly affected. You were right. She couldn't breathe. Now, none of us can. If some improvement is not seen within the next few hours, they will need to put her on a ventilator.

I cannot believe I just wrote that last sentence. My one and only child, my beautiful girl, is in trouble and all alone. I promised her I would never let that happen. Franny has camped out in her car in the hospital parking lot. I sit alone in my apartment. Both of us totally useless.

Michael is overwhelmed. After negative test results for everyone, he brought Samuel to stay with his parents. Neither of them has been out of the house for some time and is considered "safe." The reality is that I barely know Michael. But I did call and offered to do anything he might consider helpful for himself or Samuel.

I am worse at waiting than at anything else. I don't know what to do with all the energy inside of me. I can't even remember how to pray. Like you, Rachi, I am pacing. I think you do it to find answers. I'm doing it to let off steam. In this situation, there are no answers. As a result, I have also loudly and violently banged on my keyboard. I have even thrown a few things. For the first time in my life, I wish I could cry.

I thought Franny would. Cry, I mean. Instead, she has turned her fear into anger. She is mad at Michael for letting Eva wait so long. She is mad at him for bringing Samuel to his parents instead of to her. She is upset that he doesn't update her often enough. Once the anger is spent, *she* feels better. It's what she does. It's who she is.

For once, I will not begrudge cleaning up after her. I am running interference with Michael and hope he will put it all behind him when this is over. No matter what, there is no doubt that Franny loves all three of them. She wants to do something that will help but hasn't a clue what that might be. Like the rest of us, she is floundering. Perhaps, precisely because we are both in the same boat, I understand her for once. As strange as it sounds even to me, I find myself wanting to protect her as much as I want to protect everyone else.

Raffi

DEAR RAFFI,

My children went through some rough patches when they were younger, broken bones, childhood illnesses, accidents of all kinds. Throughout each trauma, the one thing I would not allow was a physical separation between us. There was not a doctor or nurse strong enough to get me to leave their side. I would be broken and shattered if I were in your position.

Perhaps you aren't aware, but I am a crier and a thrower. I would be doing plenty of both if I were you. We all have to deal in the ways that we can. I do, however, feel bad for Michael. Absorbing anger on top of everything else is a lot to ask from any young man. I'm glad you see the situation clearly enough to be there for him. I hope you can continue to be there for Franny as well. It is natural for you to feel that pull to protect her. She was an important part of your life for a number of years and continues to share the role of parent with you. No one knows better than you the depth of her love for your daughter and grandson.

When this is all over, we'll have to talk a little about this prayer thing. I'm not sure how I would have gotten through some of my life's low points if I could not turn to prayer. For now, have no fear. I will pray enough for the both of us.

I am still here as needed. I remind you that I am in the midst of my staycation and have all the time in the world to do whatever I can.

Rachi

DEAR RACHI,

The medication has begun to work and there is a marked improvement. No ventilator needed. Keep praying. The next few days will be important.

Raffi

Will do. Thank you for the good news.

Rachi

DEAR RACHI,

I breathe a long sigh of relief. Eva is home and recovering. It may take several weeks of bed rest before she will gain enough strength to begin an attempt at normalcy. We can all live with that. Samuel will remain with his other grandparents. Franny wanted to move in to take care of Eva, but Eva's doctor would not allow it. I can only imagine Michael's relief. Speaking of Michael, he is quite a fine young man. He has so far handled a huge amount of stress with an equally large amount of grace. I told Eva so the last time we spoke, which is now a daily ritual.

As the events of the last few days have transpired, I have been wondering just how much clout you have with all that praying stuff. Even God must be aware that you will never take "no" for an answer. Thank you for the prayers. More than anything, thank you for being ever-present to my need.

Speaking of need, I have been wondering why I continued a written correspondence with you when I could have simply picked up the phone and told you everything. I almost did, but then instinctively sent the text instead asking you to check your email. I believe *instinctively* is the operative word. Even in an emergency, it's what felt right. It means a lot that you followed my lead without questioning the absurdity of it.

What do you say we continue to keep up via email? It's not only a more "present" conversation, it also seems more reliable than snail mail recently. I read that there is a shortage of workers due to illness as well as greater need. Let me know what you think. I will still retain the satisfaction of putting words on paper even if the stationery is digital.

This time, without hesitation or reservation, I sign

With all my love,
Raffi

DEAR RAFFI,

I can't begin to tell you how happy I am that things turned out so well. I'll bet you can't wait to get the okay to see everyone. I'm sure they are anxious to see you as well. I guess these crises that occur in our lives give us a better glimpse of what everyone is made of. I'm glad Michael came through for everyone as did you, my friend. Sounds like you had your hands full for a while with Franny. You never know what else may have been going on in her life at the time. Maybe she was merely stretched too thin.

You know how good it feels to slip into a comfortable, worn pair of slippers after wearing dress shoes all day? I think that's what the written word was for you even though it was email rather than letters. Writing has been our comfortable way of speaking to each other. In the midst of all the new and stressful things going on in your life, adding one more new thing was simply too much. Not absurd at all.

Sounds like we (older folks) will be getting the vaccine soon. That will make a difference in how soon you can visit Eva and her family. I know there are pros and cons to getting it, but I want to put my own family at ease. The main concern all along has been the possibility of them passing Covid on to me. This way, no one will have a guilty conscience in the eventuality that I catch it, which does not seem likely after receiving the injections. Then again, who can be certain?

Yes, I have become quite comfortable with email. The part I like is that we can continue a chain of random thoughts throughout the day. It's more spontaneous. As I attempt to convince myself that it is for the sake of spontaneity, I am laughing to myself. If I am honest, there is also an ulterior motive. Random thoughts do come to me throughout the day that I wish to share, but by the time I sit down to write the letter, I have forgotten half of them. Email might be better suited for us seniors than previously thought.

However, I don't want you to think that I will be glued to my screen all day, every day. I do have a life, you know. In truth, my staycation has proved otherwise. I am bored almost to tears. These "vacation" days have been almost exactly the same as every other day. I spend most days doing what I want for all intents and purposes even if I am not vacationing. When I am working, once I have finished with therapy sessions, the rest of the time is basically my own just as it is now. However, before we were not stuck in our apartments, I walked and shopped, visited family and friends, volunteered for things at the church. The days were filled and satisfying. I have found my days are infinitely longer now. No matter how exciting the book, how captivating the movie, how tasty the meal, I remain restless.

I even tried knitting and crocheting for the umpteenth time with the same result as always. I have dozens of consecutive, tight little stitches that go on and on but turn into nothing. If this is a hobby that is supposed to be relaxing, it doesn't work. I'm nothing but frustrated. Outside of cooking, the domestic arts were never my thing. What is my thing? In my seventies and still trying to figure it out.

My one true happiness at the moment is that all is well with my children and with you.

Love,
Rachi

DEAR RACHI,

I have this sense of reliving that time in our lives when we were learning about Confession in religion class. We were taught to "examine our conscience" and recall all our sins. I've been doing that lately, only it isn't about sinning. It is more a dissection of myself, an examination of each of my many parts. Seeing ourselves clothed in embellishments and bravado is not the same as viewing ourselves in our naked truth. That is the view we get to see when we are blessed with old age. Of all times to take a keener look, we look now, when we are sagging in every direction. Of course, I am not only speaking literally of the body. I am trying honestly to see the man I am in essence.

The one thing I have come to realize is that the man I wish I was, the one I think I am, the one I sometimes pretend to be, are not the same as the one I really am.

I started reflecting on this during Eva's illness. Thinking of her and Samuel, I came to the realization that I never was a father. I can't change that by pretending now to be a grandfather, who I also am not. It isn't that I don't love them. Of course, I do. But the relationship that fatherhood is supposed to foster eludes me, my discomfort obvious to everyone involved. I don't play ball. I don't go to school plays. I don't help with homework. I never did those things with Eva, yet for a while, I believed I might do them with Samuel. It took little time to grasp the fact that I was only fooling myself, which then led me to question what else I was viewing with the same distorted lens.

My work? Do I truly wish to return to meeting deadlines, to compromising my designs to suit someone else's bizarre notion of asymmetry or flow? Do I wish to travel again on a schedule that allows time for work but none for appreciation of the setting, of the beauty, of the people? If not work, what then? What do I have left to fill the void?

The pandemic has acted as a bridge, in a way, between hyperactivity and its opposite, allowing a crossover that is gradual. I feel that a new phase is coming, but it seems to be hidden beyond a dense fog. I have no idea what is on the other side. I want to look forward to something.

Raffi

DEAREST RAFFI,

It seems we are both delving deep into our cores. I realized after my last email, that my staycation has nothing to do with what I want. Instead, it is all about what I don't want. I am tired of being strong. I am finding it harder to listen to the pain of each of my patients without letting it hurt me. It is difficult to help others cope with their loss while I am overwhelmed by mine.

This pandemic has taken away access to certain peripheral things which, of course, I miss, but it did not knock me down. I was already on the ground when it arrived.

I left my home, my surroundings, my routine. The only thing I didn't leave was the love of my life. For my entire adult life, I loved one man, one I could never leave. Instead, he left me. It was not his choice, but the result is the same. He is gone, along with the life we built together. The definition of "me" always included being part of a couple. Now I am not.

This "me" that stands alone is still a mother, a grandmother, a professional woman. What is it that leads me to be the mother I am, the grandmother I am, the professional woman? Who exactly is it that lives beneath the surface of these personas? I am no longer sure. I am in that same dense fog that surrounds you. I want to look forward to something, too.

Humor me, Raffi. Join me in playing a game.

Make a list of everywhere you would like to go.
Make a list of everything you would like to do.
Make a list of things you would like to see or hear.
Make a list of people you would like to visit.

I started doing this a few days ago. Strangely enough, it is an exercise that helps to order my priorities. Since my life has been sedentary for an extended time, getting into the full swing of things feels daunting. I find myself wishing to pick and choose; although, at first, I thought I might want to make up for lost time and do as much as I possibly could as quickly as was feasible. Now, that approach seems overwhelming. Like you, I have become accustomed to this slower pace.

This is a new aspect of aging that is rearing its ugly head. It may take much longer to develop new routines, but once we have, it is also more difficult to go back to the old ones. We have developed a new rhythm to our everyday lives, and it is becoming a pattern that is too difficult to break. We can no more return to our pre-pandemic lives as we can return to being our younger selves. What we lost this past year is gone for good.

Ergo, my lists. They give me an outline, a way in which to establish my priorities. I know I will need to cross some things off, but I will also be able to check some as doable. They may give you something to look forward to as well. I wonder if any of our items will overlap.

You will probably laugh when I tell you the first place I would like to visit. I want to go on a pilgrimage. Yes, I want to visit a holy place. It could be Lourdes or Medjugorje, Guadalupe or Fatima. I am not searching for a physical cure for anything. I badly want to feel sacred ground. I wish to stand on it. I want to absorb it. Fatima is my first choice.

How about you?

Waiting,
Rachi

P.S. You didn't mention Eva in your last email. I assume that means her recovery is proceeding well. I'm still sending prayers to your lovely city.

MY DEAR FRIEND,

I paint this letter as a sunrise at earliest dawn. Night is just receding, and the sun barely peeks. Most of the canvas remains dark.

You are correct in your assumption. Eva is making slow but steady progress. Samuel will be returning home soon. Seems daily life is beginning to normalize.

Well, Rachi, you always surprise me. I would never have guessed that your heart is longing for the sacred. You have always been somewhat permeable. You used to have good feelings and bad feelings about things. I remember that architectural tour we went on once. You left one of the houses as quickly as you could because you "felt" something bad had happened there. Later we found out someone had been murdered, right in that kitchen, thirty years before! I pretended to laugh it off, but you scared the hell out of me.

You are probably the same way with your patients, and I think I understand why you needed a break from the therapy sessions. Missing your life with Matt reminds me of something else. It's like your tongue constantly touching a sore tooth. It's as if you need to reassure yourself that the pain is still there, all the while wishing it would go away. If you don't mind my assuming your role for a brief observation, I would like to say that you are allowed to let go of the pain. It does not mean you love him less. Don't allow your sense of loyalty to those you care about keep you from moving on with your life. Remember that it *is* your life. Even when you were part of a couple, it was still *your* life.

Anyway, I can certainly understand your desire and need to feel good vibes. I feel the same way myself. I have paid little attention to religion or miracles in my life, but from the little I know, I think Fatima is an excellent choice. I've never been to Portugal. Besides, isn't that where our good old Mateus comes from?

There are many places in this world I have never been, and for the most part, I have no desire to change that. I would, however, without hesitation return to some of my favorite places. There is one in Italy, Sirmione on Lake Garda. I went there the first time on your recommendation, so I know you like it also. After purifying our souls in Fatima, we could give our bodies the pleasures of sun, and water, and wonderful meals of freshly caught fish, just picked vegetables and fruit, and that marvelous *gelato*. A little yin for you, a little yang for me. I could look forward to that.

What do you think?

Raffi

My Dear Friend,

Have you put your foot in your mouth, or do you mean it? Are you suggesting we travel together once it is allowed again?

Just asking,
Rachi

RACHI,

I thought it through before sending the message. Could this emailing be making me crazy? Not sure about that. I am sure about the suggestion. I want to see you and spend real time with you. Wouldn't a trip be the perfect way? We could go to Portugal first and then on to Garda. I have been thinking that by the time everyone is vaccinated and things open up again, it will probably be off season for these places, which is even better, not so much for the money, but for the crowds.

Do you remember that inn you referred me to in Sirmione? We can try there again. The rooms were tiny, but they all had balconies overlooking the lake. And when you walked out of the inn, you found yourself across the courtyard from that fantastic little restaurant that had about three tables. You could sit at a table in the courtyard and almost touch the water as you drank a morning espresso. I can take care of the Italy part of the trip if you handle the Portugal part.

What do you say?

Make me a happy man,
Raffi

DEAR RAFFI,

I can't believe I'm saying this, but "yes." Absolutely, yes. After all these years of not seeing each other, to take a trip together seems surreal. I must admit, I am thrilled. I can't wait to start planning. Let's try for October. Do you think that gives the world enough time to recover?

I apologize for taking so long to answer such an important question, but I received my first vaccine a few days ago. I got a migraine from hell as the sole but debilitating side effect. I have been in bed for several days, and looking at a computer screen was out of the question. I'm fine now, and I guess it is a small price to pay for the peace of mind I feel. Do you have an appointment yet for your vaccine? I am extremely happy to hear about Eva and her family. The worst seems to be behind them. I'm sure she will be thrilled to have Samuel back home. That alone should expedite her recovery.

I gave some thought to your concept of what fatherhood is all about. All those things you said you never did were also never done by your father or mine. Our fathers were working when those activities were taking place. I can't speak for you, but I ended up having a great relationship with my father even without his presence at everything. When he wasn't working, almost all his time was spent with family. I knew I could always go to him if I needed anything. I never once doubted that he loved me. When I became an adult, we were pretty good friends. We could talk about anything.

Could be that's where you shine, as an adult father. Talk to Eva. Talk to her about anything that she wants to talk about. Find something that interests her and figure out a way to share it. I learned all about football for one of my sons, and it's still the conversation opener. From there, we roam around to all kinds of topics. But you first need something to rev the engine.

I'll begin to scope out what is happening in Fatima and what October looks like. Is there anything else in Portugal you want to see? Let me know.

I'm excited!!!
Rachi

SWEET RACHI,

Remember the last letter I painted? The one with the sun just peeking through? It's up and shining bright at last.

I think we should go to Porto as well as Fatima. It's a coastal town. It's famous for port wine as you may have guessed. It has a thriving restaurant scene and is not as touristy as Lisbon, which is another place we might want to see. How long is this trip going to be? That's the first decision we have to make before I start scoping things out. I would be happy with a week in each country. I haven't taken such a long vacation since one of my honeymoons. I can't remember which one.

Your thoughts on fatherhood eased my conscience a little. It is true about our own fathers. Our fathers worked a lot, but when they weren't working, everything else they did included family. I did have a good relationship with my father, considering how little time we spent with each other. My mom, as you know, was a black hole for everyone's time. She was a genius at taking.

You, my dear, are the psychologist. Tell me. Did I keep marrying my mother? It wasn't until I wrote that last paragraph that it ever occurred to me. So many of the women in my life have been experts at taking. And just like that little boy so many years ago, trying so hard to please his mother, I could never give them enough. What an epiphany!

Eva is not like that. Neither are you. I knew there was a reason I love you both the best.

Your suddenly enlightened,
Raffi

MY DEAR BRUISED RAFFI,

An epiphany indeed. I hesitate to blur the lines of our friendship with any kind of psychoanalysis, but I will tell you that you hit the jackpot. The home lives of our childhood are a major influence on the decisions of our adulthood. The challenge is seeing ourselves as we were then—children—a realization that then allows us to extend to ourselves some degree of understanding and compassion.

From what you've shared with me, I know your mother suffered from emotional problems that were so little understood back then. She was not taking out of greed, but out of overwhelming need. Not your father as an adult nor you as a child could ever have given enough to change that situation. Any pain that resulted was, in a way, nobody's fault. It just was.

I will purposely and with great effort refrain from commenting on your marriages. I am happy that Eva does not fit the pattern of other women in your life, and that you have excluded me as well. We two are your present, after all. The others are past, hopefully lessons learned, but for sure nothing you can change.

How exciting for me. I will be traveling not only with an old friend, but with a new, enlightened one, as well.

Two weeks sound perfect. I have one question for you before I start making plans. Do you wish to rent a car and drive? If not, I will check train routes, etc. Porto is a good idea. I have learned of a direct plane route to Porto from the Newark airport. Does that sound doable to you? I only know La Guardia and JFK. Input, please.

Rachi

P.S. I just found out that Vila Real, the baroque palace that was pictured on the label of Mateus, our favorite rosé, is located in the

Province of Tras-os-Montes, a three-hour drive from Porto. It might be too long a distance to travel for purely sentimental reasons, but perhaps there are other interesting sites to visit nearby that might make it worth our while. That's a little excursion we can play by ear.

DEAR RACHI,

You are so diplomatic. Thank you for seeing my family dysfunction with such kind eyes. Sometimes I'm amazed that I turned out as well as I did despite my many mistakes. I gladly offer my father full credit for that. It is only recently that I have begun to understand what his life must have been like. I remember sadness at times, but never anger. There must have been a great love between my parents despite everything. I envy them that.

Speaking of my wives (which I know you currently decline to do, but I don't), Franny seems to have caused more damage than I thought. Apparently, Michael has a boiling point, and she helped him reach it. Some words were exchanged that are now out there and can't be erased. They have retreated to their respective corners, placing Eva right in the middle. Franny's current husband has remained uninvolved, probably for the sake of self-preservation. Eva suggested I stay out of it, too, but I decided to call Michael on the sly. I thought it appropriate to offer a shoulder, a little sympathy based on understanding the woman involved. I didn't make excuses for her. I only reinforced that her heart is in the right place, even when that very heart seems difficult to locate. In the end, Michael thanked me, and we decided to keep the conversation between "us boys." Bet you never saw me as the peacemaker.

You, of all people, should know that I was born with a steering wheel in my hands. Of course, I want to drive. I would go crazy waiting for trains that don't arrive on schedule and putting up with crowds and crying babies. Not for me. After you arrange the city stays, I will arrange for the car and the proper English-speaking GPS. I promise we will not get lost unless we want to. We might even want to chance a trip to that Mateus palace you mentioned. Who knew it was a real place?

I almost forgot. I had another brilliant idea. I think you should fly to New York and then leave together with me for the longer, second stretch. The transatlantic part will be much more fun to do together rather than with some random stranger who places his arm on your armrest for ten hours or whatever.

Come the day before we leave for Europe, and you can spend the night here. Any of the airports we depart from, including the one in Newark, will be easy to get to by cab or ride-share. If it is at all possible to book an afternoon flight, we can begin our little escapade slow and easy.

I will not take no for an answer.

Your determined companion,
Raffi

MY DEAR ELITIST FRIEND,

I had no idea that you are not a man for the masses. I got a chuckle out of everything you said because I am exactly the same way. Matt and I drove everywhere we could and for the same reason. We never felt comfortable being tied down to schedules and having to share our experiences with strangers. I was the navigator (before GPS) with my trusty road maps, and he was always the driver. We used to pack picnic lunches and then take off in a different direction each day no matter what country we were in. We found some of the loveliest places that way. Hopefully, you and I will be as lucky.

Here are some pertinent details about distances. Fatima is seventy-six miles from Lisbon and just over one hundred miles from Porto. I suggest we fly into Porto on that direct flight from Newark and stay there several days, then drive to Fatima and book a hotel there for two or three nights. After Fatima we drive back to Porto for a flight to Milan (very short and under $50.00). In Milan we pick up another rental and drive to Sirmione which should take less than two hours (about 85mi.) We can return to the States from Milan. What I need to know is how many nights to book for each destination and if you also want to squeeze Lisbon in there somewhere.

As far as your un-flexible invitation to cohabitate on the night before we leave, I accept. I accept with gratitude, in fact, as it will break up the flight time a little for me. Unless we decide to fly to Lisbon instead of Porto. There is a direct flight there from Chicago. But doing the bulk of the flight together sounds like a better plan. I know you mentioned two weeks, but I am putting a full three weeks aside, so you can take that into consideration when thinking about Lisbon and the rest of the timing.

You must be mellowing in your senior years. Ordinarily, I would expect you not to get involved in the drama of your ex and your son-in-law. I know you did it for Eva. And you think you're not a good father! Once Eva feels well enough to resume her usual position in that trio, I'm sure things will relax between Franny and Michael. With time, everything will be back to normal. It seems recovery time is quite unique to each patient. I hope Eva is being good to herself and allowing her body to heal at its own pace.

By the way, have you told anyone yet about our plans? I'll bet they don't even know who I am.

Let me know how that goes.

A presto,
Rachi

DEAREST RACHI,

I just received my first vaccine. No problems to speak of, so I am halfway to seeing Eva and Samuel. Eva is recovering well. More than anything, she is a bit stir crazy, a little like her father after all. She also feels guilty about not having the stamina to do as much with Samuel; although, it sounds as if he has been quite a trooper throughout.

I am looking forward to having a roommate even if for one night. Can you believe the last time that happened with us was the night I slept on your family's sofa to pull one of our famous all-nighters back in our school days? If I remember correctly, you were never a fan of mornings, so I hope you are able to book afternoon or evening flights.

Depending on flight times, let's stay the first night in Porto so we can un-jetlag and then drive to Fatima. We'll book two nights there and go back to Porto for four more nights. That way, we can explore at our own pace. Garda should prove even more relaxing. All I want to do is eat good food, take long walks, and talk. I know that doesn't sound ambitious, but to me it sounds like heaven. Go ahead and book the flights and the Portugal hotels; then I'll call the inn in Sirmione and plan for the cars, as well. As far as I'm concerned, no need to squeeze in another city.

Speaking of heaven, we should also avoid the news. By then, I will have had more than my share of garish, unbelievable headlines. With so much devastation around us, why on earth do people give so much importance to some pseudo-celebrity with an empty space between his or her ears? Someone pulls a topic out of the sky, declares himself or herself an expert on it, and the whole world listens with bated breath. Why on earth do we care? It would be kind to attribute this attention to a need to escape the reality of our own world, but it says more about the flock of "followers" that we have become. Of itself, that might not be a bad thing. It is who we choose to follow that is the problem.

You have more children and grandchildren than I. Is there hope for those generations? Do they ever look up from those screens and see what is around them? Do they ever pull the earbuds out and listen to another human being, a bird, the sound of the wind? God, I hope so.

Your game with the lists has led me to these thoughts. I have been thinking about what else I want to do or see besides our travel. Who else do I want to visit or reconnect with? So far, the lists are not long.

I'll show you mine if you show me yours.

Love,
Raffi

DEAR RAFFI,

Holy cow, what a wealth of topics was in your last email. I hardly know where to begin.

Let me start with the practical. If nothing changes regarding Covid, we will leave from Newark on Saturday, October 2 for Porto where we will arrive on Sunday, October 3. We can drive to Fatima the next day. There I have booked rooms for October 4 through 6. On Thursday the 7th, we will return to Porto where we are booked through the 9th.

On Sunday the 10th we depart for Milan, drive to Sirmione and stay through the 15th. On Saturday the 16th, we drive back to Milan where we hop a flight back to New York. I will catch a connecting flight there at JFK to return to Chicago.

All you need to do is take care of the hotel in Italy and arrange for the autos of your choice in each locale. And prepare your guest room, of course, for Friday, October 1. My flight arrives late afternoon at La Guardia and I can take a taxi from there. I think that should take care of everything. The butterflies are finally starting. I can't believe I will truly be knocking on your door soon!

By the way, did you ever replace or refinish your door? You were planning to make a statement with it, and I've been wondering what it will say.

I have to start planning my wardrobe. I have, in the past, been told that I tend to overpack. I am making a concerted effort not to do so this time. I think I can make it with one bag and one carry-on.

I have had my second vaccine and begun to venture out more this past week. A trip to the beauty salon was one of my first outings, so I feel like a new woman. A mani/pedi can do wonders.

My lists are not long either. I have seen and done much in my life. Some things I might have desired when I was younger don't hold the same allure now. What I plan to do as soon as it is possible is to attend plays, live concerts, and operas. I will find it beyond satisfying to attend a Mass and receive Communion, as well.

That reminds me of your question about the next generations. You and I both received Catholic educations throughout our school years. On the surface, that seems as if it should limit our thought process. Instead, I find it does the exact opposite. Although most things were presented within the context of Catholic doctrine, we were taught how to think for ourselves. I remember doubting much of that doctrine itself during a particular phase of my life. In so doing, I was merely following the pattern I had been taught. I was trained to think it all through even if the end conclusion would end up being not a matter of thought at all, but of faith, instead. All my life I have tried to think things through; I have attempted to distinguish between fact and opinion and then arrive at my own conclusions.

I believe this is precisely the issue with which we are now dealing. Everything that should be presented as an op-ed is, instead, offered as if it is factual reporting. The lines between facts and opinions blur and blend right into each other. When we were younger, we questioned what Nixon said as well as what Johnson said. We didn't care that one was a Republican and one a Democrat. Neither one of their addresses to the nation was taken as Gospel truth, and they were presidents of the United States, leaders of the Free World. Today, an entertainer, a sports figure, a billionaire CEO is "important" enough to start a boycott or a riot. Throw social media into the mix and the creepy kid next door that lives in his mother's basement can do the same thing. Then there will be dozens of readers who will offer their own two cents. But again, for the most part, that will be more opinions. Yet in the meantime, many others will act based on what one of these people said while saving the questions and fact-checking for later, their own opinions not based on anything substantive.

On the other hand, we are bombarded with so much information that it is impossible to filter through it all. I know a lot of people that are simply overwhelmed. They narrow their field of interest and entire thought process to one or two topics and follow only those and sort-of ignore everything else. For young people it may be music or movies or games. By concentrating on fewer things, they are not so stressed out. However, their world becomes limited. These are usually the people that can't tell the difference between a country and a city, or haven't the faintest idea who their senator is, or what D-Day was all about. All their focus has been on only one or two areas of interest for so long that they aren't aware that other things exist let alone may be important.

What do I think about the younger generations? I think these are tough times. I think the world as we knew it no longer exists. Whereas, we, at our age, can stand back and observe, they can't. They have to live in it. I hope someone can find a better way for them to do that, one that doesn't involve mind altering drugs, alcohol, or violence. I think family is a great place to start. If we could only be families again. And don't underestimate the fact that most of our teachers were nuns! You can make all the jokes you want about them and their "rulers," but they knew how to keep us focused, and they were always available for extra help.

I have many friends our age who assumed they had shown by example the importance of family, faith, and, to a certain extent, discipline. Now they see the way their children are raising their grandchildren with what appears to be a completely different set of values. There is no family dinner. No church on Sunday. They hear conversations between their children and grandchildren that show a lack of respect on both sides. Sadly, sometimes they find themselves pushed aside as totally irrelevant. So many of my conversations with these friends make me sad. Most of them are perpetually questioning themselves. They feel that they are the ones that somehow failed.

I, personally, am not sure who exactly is to blame. I have one friend, Lizzy, whose daughter hasn't spoken to her in over five years. Lizzy is sweet and kind and easy to get along with. Another friend, Ruth, can be a royal pain. She demands a lot from her children and grandchildren yet is included in everything they do. I know I'm in the business of figuring people out, but the only things I know for sure are that people are complex and complicated. They are who they are as a result of so many things. Perhaps Lizzy has mellowed over the years and was not as gentle with her daughter as she now is with others. And maybe Ruth shares other characteristics with her children and grandchildren which somehow balance out the more abrasive behavior.

I only wish there were a way to freeze-frame today's youth somehow. Get them to stop for a little while—stop listening, stop talking, stop doing. Just be quiet for a moment. Just be.

OMG. Look how I have gone on and on and on. Sorry. Remember, you asked.

I'll be quiet now.

Love,
Rachi

Email

DEAREST RACHI,

I am sketching a baseball field. Let's call it Sox Park. The batter is at the plate looking at the pitcher. The nine players on the field are all holding their positions. They all look exactly like the pitcher. All nine players on the team are you. You waiting to catch that ball. You daring the batter to hit that pitch. And in that instant, all ten players on that field know that today, the opposing team will not score, and that both teams will bear witness to the rarity of a perfect game.

There it is, that fire, that passion that was you in our younger days. The more we share, the more I find that not much has changed. Certainly, your own life experiences have molded your personality to some extent, but only to some extent. The basic parameters have remained the same. You are still a keen observer as well as a hopeful crusader. You may think you want to remain on the sidelines, but you won't. We talked before about you as the coach coming up with the plays but not actively implementing them yourself on the field as part of the team. If you saw a way to reach your children, your grandchildren, to impart to them something of importance (as you said earlier about childhood emergency room visits), then there isn't a force in this world strong enough to hold you back. You wouldn't even need the backing of the rest of the team. You would be on that field with or without them, playing every position if you had to. Being the troublemaker that I am, I would dare anyone to try to stop you just so I could sit back and watch you win every time.

You mentioned that neither you nor the world was the same anymore. Judging from your letters, I would have to disagree. Your basic character, your core personality, seem, in fact, comfortably the same. Of course, you have matured, gained in wisdom. You have been tempered by sorrow and lightened by joy. Some change is inevitable.

In all honesty, this was my only concern about meeting again after all these years. I was worried you might have changed too much, that I would no longer know you. I was concerned that the patterns of your life might have changed you so much we would no longer "click." With every letter I read, more and more dissuades that fear.

The fear replacing it is how much I have changed. My cup runneth over with professional satisfaction. That same cup runs dry with personal fulfillment. I put all my energy and creativity into my work with nothing left for anything else. I feel like those people you mentioned that have one-track minds and can handle information about only one thing at a time. The interesting part is that, until now, I never felt as if I was missing anything. Now, with such a diminished workload, I am lost.

Perhaps, this trip will help me find myself. You can help me look, or am I asking too much? Could it be that you are also looking for something? Fatima is not, after all, the first destination that comes to mind for fun in the sun. Is there something in your life that requires a miraculous transformation? Could it actually be, as you mentioned before, that we are both becoming too aware of our approaching mortality? Do we both wish to return to our youth and *re-transform*, eliminate all the years in between, filled with responsibility and obligation? Go back to a time when we stopped listening, and talking, and doing, and just were?

Or, perhaps it is nothing more than a dreary, rainy day in New York. I'm told the lack of sunshine can do strange things.

I know! I will place my order for dinner and nurse a Manhattan while I wait for it to arrive. I'll return after eating. My mood will be better then, I promise.

True to my word, I am back and better than ever. (In addition to the Manhattan, I had wine with dinner!) Thank goodness for that. The delivery boy got lost. You might ask, "How could that happen when the restaurant is only three doors away?" The answer is, "It's my door again." There is currently no number on it. The young man did not get lost until he was inside my building. He took the elevator down to the lobby three times before he was able to figure things out. Luckily the food was still warm enough, or perhaps I no longer cared since I was pouring my third glass of wine by then. Anyway, this particular restaurant is finally delivering again to my building. Its menu is standard American fare, and the quality is good. I had a large, juicy, medium-rare steak burger with all the trimmings including fries and slaw. It was exactly what I needed. Everything about my mood is better, and while I could delete the previous part of this email, I am leaving it so that you can see the effect a good meal has on me.

Now I can confirm that the autos are rented for Portugal and Italy, and we have two small adjoining rooms in Sirmione on the second floor, each with its own balcony overlooking the water. We are set to go.

I plan to tell Eva and give her our itinerary just before we leave. It may be the first time I travel since Covid, and that might be of some concern. I prefer not to have to discuss it for months in advance. How about you? Do you anticipate any trepidation from your children?

How much do you know about Portuguese food? I designed a seafood restaurant in Boston that offered a Portuguese menu. I'll tell you about it in my next email.

Good night, dear.
Raffi

Dear Raffi,

Delivery service isn't quite so easy where I live, but after your last email, I got in the car and drove to the nearest takeout and ordered a burger and fries. You made yours sound so good! I thoroughly enjoyed mine, too.

Funny about your delivery getting lost. What is going on with your door? Did you ever check the condo rules about color, frescos, etc.? Sounds as though it has become quite a project.

Why do you assume that you missed something in your life even though you never felt the loss? Perhaps you didn't feel it because it wasn't there. Maybe in hindsight you're asking too much. You said yourself that you put "all" of your energy into your profession. That implies there wasn't any left over. That is the genius and the curse of immersing yourself in something. Sometimes, there is nothing left over. I see it often in persons with a vocation rather than a profession. I'm not sure it's possible to have more than one vocation at a time.

No longer having as much work may mean that it is time for a new chapter in your life. You do have the energy and creativity for something else. I don't think any of this is about a miraculous transformation. It's just life.

If you recall, shortly before Eva was taken ill, I had begun a staycation, remaining in my condo, but not "working." I didn't do that on a whim. I did it out of desperation. It was becoming more and more difficult to listen to and hope to help them, other people, while feeling overwhelmed by my own issues. The Covid isolation was getting to me, and I found myself frequently fighting off my own depression. I knew I needed time for myself, but too much time to myself seemed to be the problem to begin with.

My work, like yours, took up the better part of my time since my children were in their teens. Like you, I have always loved it and found it satisfying and fulfilling. What I came recently to realize is that it is also draining, and that I had no reserve resources, resources I needed to confront all the losses and changes in my own life. You, my dear friend, are not the only one who is lost.

However, I am not going to Fatima for a miracle. Remember that saying that's attributed to Einstein? "There are two ways to live your life. One is as though nothing is a miracle. The other is as though everything is a miracle." I have witnessed miracles all my life. They have filled me with wonder and awe, with gratitude and faith. Those same feelings have been felt by hundreds of thousands of pilgrims on that soil since the first apparition occurred. I believe that by standing on that sacred soil I will absorb at least some of those same feelings. My own personal miracles were "small," a window opening when a door closed. Yet, when I recognized it for what it was, it felt wonderful. Imagine breathing in the feeling of the big things that happened in Fatima. The sun fell to earth, for God's sake! I know. I know. Scientists can always find a way to explain the phenomenon. But even if certain things aligned in such a way to provoke a scientific occurrence, why then, why on that day, at that specific time? I understand that for some, even looking at it in this way does not change their minds. I'm not interested in changing anyone's mind. I know it is a matter of faith. I hope this doesn't sound silly, but for me, sometimes it is the complete opposite. Things that should be matters of faith are the ones I "know" to be true. This is a topic that should keep us going for the entire flight, at least one way, unless you are one of those people that can fall asleep anywhere.

I have already told my children about our trip. About our friendship they already knew. Matt and I have told them all kinds of stories over the years about our times together. I think they are relieved to know that I'm not traveling alone.

Portuguese food. I don't know much about it beyond the generic Mediterranean diet aspect of it. I can't wait for you to share. That Portuguese restaurant must have been a fun project. Strange to say, I've never been to Boston.

Be safe,
Rachi

MY POOR DEPRIVED RACHI,

Perhaps after our first trip, we should plan others to cities in our own country that we have never seen. I'm sorry you have so far missed Boston. I think you would like it. As you probably already know, many Portuguese immigrants to the U.S. settled on the East Coast. Whatever their reasons for leaving their birth place, they found there a coastal area that provided much the same type of labor they were accustomed to in their own fishing villages. They brought with them their language, their Roman Catholic religion, their customs, and, of course, their food, which became the mainstay of the restaurant that I helped design in Boston.

Allow me to say, without a doubt, that Portuguese food is fantastic. Needless to say, much of the cuisine incorporates fish. Salt cod, or *bacalhau*, is an important one, as is octopus, known as *polvo*. They turn several things into fritters or croquettes and encase others as empanadas, which originated in Portugal, by the way. Lunch might be *caldo verde* which is a kale soup, or *bifanas,* which are sandwiches of thinly sliced pork. A typical breakfast might include bread, butter, ham, cheese, and jam. And they have a ubiquitous dessert called *pateis de nata,* a custard tart. They also supposedly do marvelous things with innards such as tripe, but if you don't mind, I prefer to stay away from that one. Bottom line, I have a feeling we will be eating well in both countries. We'll need plenty of walks to keep from gaining weight. This Covid inertia has already messed enough with my waistline.

It occurred to me after your last email that my family believes my life began in New York. There was little contact with relatives back in Chicago. There was no estrangement, merely a drifting away with sporadic contact. Eva had met my parents only a few times before my mother died. Once she was gone, my father spent his time in Arizona happy to have some peace at last, but surprisingly missing her more than he could have thought possible. As you know, he died a few years later. Eva has no idea what my childhood and adolescence were like. I worked so hard at forgetting the bad part that I succeeded in temporarily forgetting it all. Now, I'm sorry I never told her about you and how we met on that first day at university. I'm not sure how we ended up in three gen-ed classes together, or how we ended up always sitting next to each other, but I'm sure it must have been one of the small miracles you mentioned in your last email. You were the bright star I could have hung my memories on. And, of course, Matt. You and Matt and me, although you didn't meet Matt until the following year. I plan to show Eva pictures and tell her stories after our trip. We'll give her some newer memories to buttress the old.

I am finally going to visit them all next weekend. Michael and Eva are back to work remotely for the most part, and Samuel is also remote for preschool. I was invited for dinner, an actual home-cooked meal. I am looking forward to it. Will tell you all about it next time.

I have to paint my door all one color. It may have a knocker, so long as it is brass, but no other decoration (although wreaths are permitted at Christmas and menorahs for Hanukkiah, without the lit candles, of course). The door knobs and numbers must be purchased at a specific establishment so they can be uniform (also brass). So, no frescos, no creativity, no free reign to my imagination.

My door used to be black so the damage was very obvious. It is in the process of being stripped down to bare wood since black is difficult to paint-over. It will be repainted as soon as I decide on a new color, which for some reason, is proving to be a more difficult task than I thought. I have surreptitiously walked the corridors on two floors to help give me ideas. So far, I have found monotony, lots and lots of the same.

I wish you had mentioned sooner that you were feeling down. I'm sorry it happened exactly at the moment I was not there for you. I suppose I mistakenly assumed that you were *finished* with your grieving, as if that could possibly be true. And, until you mentioned it, I guess I also gave no thought to all the other things you have lost. Your letters and emails keep buoying up my ego or offering perspective, and for that, I thank you. But I would be grateful to be given the opportunity to reciprocate, anytime, anywhere. All you have to do is ask.

Love,
Raffi

DEAR RAFFI,

I am happy to hear you are visiting with your family at last. I'm sure it won't matter at all what the dinner tastes like. You have waited so long and been so filled with worry. Your concern, of course, was well-founded under the circumstances.

Thank God it is behind you, as is your entire life before New York, apparently. I am astounded that you shared none of it with Eva or others that were part of your life after your move. To some extent I understand. I remember how difficult some days were for you although you seldom chose to talk about it. Looking back now, I realize those were the days we often chose to cut class. You were too restless to sit still. We used to hop in your car and drive to the lakefront, or we might decide to walk even in the dead of winter to that hot dog stand that was blocks away. They did have the best "Chicago dogs" of anywhere I have tried since, and I can't even remember its name. Sometimes, we just sat in one of the school lounges and talked about anything except whatever had happened in your world the night before. It feels strange to be associated with all those bad memories, but on the other hand, I am glad I was there. Many of those *escapes* turned into carefree moments of great fun. Those are memories you could definitely share.

You made the Portuguese food sound fantastic. I'm with you all the way on the tripe and any other innards that show up on the menu. Let's be sure we know the Portuguese words for heart, and lungs, and liver, and brains. I like knowing what's on my plate before I consume it.

Thank you for offering me your shoulder if ever I need one. I am good at listening, not so good at sharing. I had a mentor in my field to whom I could always go for help, not only to consult about a difficult case, but also to seek help for myself. I had the utmost faith in her wisdom as well as her discretion. I knew anything we discussed would remain between us. That privacy is extremely important to me.

Unfortunately, her presence in my life is another one of my losses. She died suddenly, a mere five months after Matt's death. Since then, I have kept my feelings to myself. Please don't expect a sudden divulging of all my secrets. Old habits die hard. It may take a while to get comfortable, but I am happy to know I have an option, an outlet, a safe place.

On that grateful note, I wish you a Happy Easter.

Love,
Rachi

P.S. I suggest hot pink for your door. Shake things up a bit.

Dear Rachi,

I wish you a Happy Easter, as well. I hope you will be spending it with family. I am excited to be seeing Eva, Michael, and Samuel next weekend even if not for Easter, which they are celebrating with Michael's family. I will feel better when I can see Eva's face and know for sure that she is okay.

You spoke about sharing in your last email. Seems we both have that problem. At least I had it when we were younger. You are correct. I had difficulty staying in class particularly when my mother was having an episode. As you noted, I was not interested in talking about it, only being distracted from it. I was embarrassed half the time, literally *half* the time. My mother was two different people, and only one of them was presentable, the one she was about half the time. I never knew which one she would be on any given day. I'm sure you remember that my father and my uncle, one of my mother's brothers, bore the brunt of caring for her, leaving me to fend for myself. I told you and Matt all this in bits and pieces, but most of our other friends never knew any of it. Although I was often ashamed, she had this special something that I couldn't help but love. There were times I thought there was something wrong with me *because* I loved her. Then I realized she had the same effect on my father, on her brother, and on anyone else that knew her. And then I was ashamed of myself for keeping her hidden all that time.

Upon reflection, I understand why I kept my distance from anything that had to do with that period of my life. Even if you choose not to parse my words with a professional, clinical analysis, you will still see my youth, at the very least, as complicated. So, I left Chicago behind me and moved on. Neither Eva nor any of my wives ever knew my parents except in passing, casually, on the periphery of social occasions.

Speaking of sharing, I will be sharing Easter dinner with another "senior" gentleman that lives in my building. He is a former travel writer for one of the major publications. He's an excellent storyteller and not half-bad as a cook, so I anticipate an enjoyable evening. The last time we were together for a meal, he was in his French period and prepared an excellent *coq au vin*. I will be grateful this year for a good, old-fashioned, American smoked ham with a tasty potato dish and a nice salad. I just want to see a human countenance at the other end of the table.

Buona Pasqua.
Raffi

P.S. Looking at paint samples right now. Not finding a palatable hot pink. Whatever I choose I do not plan to reveal. This way, you'll be surprised when you get here.

Dear Raffi,

Easter was the first holiday last year that families were unable to celebrate together. Who would have dreamed that we would still be dealing with masking and distancing problems one year later? I did spend the day with one of my sons. Everyone in his household is vaccinated as am I, so we felt comfortable having dinner together. Some of the others came after dinner and remained masked and six feet away. It was not the best but better than last year.

My daughter-in-law insisted that I get a break from the cooking and prepared the entire meal herself. The dinner was nice with traditional Easter dishes including a beautiful baked ham with all the trimmings. Everything was well-prepared and tasty, so I feel guilty saying this and would never mention it to anyone else, but I missed the pasta course. For some reason, especially for Easter, the absent Italian food traditions made it seem less of a holiday. When my parents were hosting, even when Matt and I were hosting, we had hams and turkey on various holidays and made sure to honor the "American" traditions. But we also added pasta, meatballs, *braciola*, and fresh artichokes. I know it isn't only the food that makes the holiday, but it sure is an important part. No matter how filled the plates are now, without the foods connecting all the memories, they somehow still look empty.

Also, don't get me started on the "meaning of Easter." My youngest grandchildren have no clue that Easter is a religious holiday. Then what is the point?

Have I officially become an old fogey? Tell me it isn't so.

Love,
Rachi

DEAR RACHI,

I am back to painting my letters. This time I have drawn tables, beautifully decorated tables, set with sparkling crystal and exquisite china, lit candles, hams and side dishes, baskets of bread, pitchers of water and carafes of wine. Many guests are seated. Some are laughing and others are glaring and pointing fingers.

I'm not sure whether to be angry about it or just laugh. Sorry to skip your entire Easter conundrum, but Eva invited Franny and her husband for dinner on the same night that they invited me. She probably thought she was defusing an awkward situation. Michael probably figured he was fulfilling his obligation with all the old geezers at once. (Eva confided that he had already consumed one Manhattan before we arrived, with Samuel, once again, enjoying the cherry.) It was not the cozy family dinner I had hoped for, especially after I became the scapegoat.

Rather than direct her snide remarks toward Michael, Franny threw them my way. At one point, they turned to pity for my bachelor state during a pandemic. Did I not feel awful finding myself completely alone? Without my work, what did I do all day? What would become of me after the lockdown with no projects or future plans? Tsk. Tsk. Was I reaping what I sowed?

I lied. I do hope you are sitting down.

I introduced them, in a matter of speaking, to the love of my life—

You.

Are you still there?

I couldn't help myself. I couldn't stand the attitude of superiority and the nonsense that went with it. I told them about our trip and how I have waited all my life to take it with you, my one true love.

It stopped her in her tracks. Once it hit her that I might have loved you *while* I was married to her, she quickly fell off her high horse. In one fell swoop, you have been outed not only as the love of my life, but also as a home-wrecker. I painted you as a free spirit who had no desire to tie herself down with the conventionality of a marriage, not then, not now.

I could feel Franny studying me, seeing me in a whole new light, searching for other tidbits she might not know about me.

I kept imagining her rushing home, rummaging through old boxes in the basement, frantically seeking any incriminating correspondence I may have left behind.

As we left, I whispered to Eva that I had made it up. I'm not sure at this point exactly what she believes, and she is the only one I care about.

Except you, of course. I hope you aren't angry. After all, it wasn't all a lie. In a way, you are the love of my life. You're the only one who has always been there. You're the only one who is here now. At least I hope you are. Don't be mad. Take your time to write back.

Sheepishly,
Raffi

Email

RAFFI,

How could you? Tell me you are joking. I know I will probably never meet any of these people, but I'm embarrassed anyway. You didn't give them my name, did you?

A little steamed,
Rachi

Darling Rachi,

I could tell you I was joking about the whole thing, but it would be another lie. The devil made me do it—the one inside my crazy ex-wife. Ex-spouses are something you can't understand unless you have one. They are always trying to prove that they were right in walking away or that you were wrong in doing so. Either way, they have to show you up. They have to be the ones that ended up with a better life.

Next, you're going to ask me why I still care. Ordinarily, I don't. But last night's competition was for Eva's sake. I will not be demeaned in front of my only child.

At least that was what I was trying to prevent. In retrospect, I guess I accomplished the exact opposite. Now she thinks I was disloyal even during that small period when we were supposed to be a family.

I promise I will call Eva today and clarify everything for her. But first, I will swear her to secrecy. Let Franny think for a while about something other than messing with Eva and Michael, who, by the way, I believe was secretly enjoying every minute of the *Franny fluster.*

I will also promise never to introduce you to Franny. You will never have to be treated like "the other woman." Although in a way, you always have been.

Contritely,
Raffi

DEAR RAFFI,

You are not at all contrite, and I barely know where to begin. Since when has your ego been so fragile, especially in regards to Eva? Everything you've written about her points to her being "daddy's little girl."

Don't forget that Franny needs to make up for the discord between herself and Michael. She might be the insecure one, so maybe you could try to be a little kinder instead of reinforcing that insecurity.

I will give her one thing, though. She knows you. She knows how to push your buttons. And you know her well enough to know how to exact your revenge.

Chalk it up to having a little fun with them. Tell everyone the truth, and then let it go. You can tell them or not about our trip and our friendship. But tell them the truth about the past.

When you're done with that, please tell me in what way you think I have always been "the other woman"? Now, you even have me wondering.

In the hope of soon regaining my untarnished reputation,
Rachi

DEAR RACHI,

All right. Done. All amends have been made albeit in a somewhat cowardly fashion. I explained everything to Eva and then asked her to pass it on. After she stopped laughing, she agreed. I had already told Eva it was a joke, but now Franny will also know the truth and can stop wondering about the past. In addition, your name and honor have been restored.

I did tell Eva that the trip is real and that I am traveling with a friend. They can all assume whatever they want from that.

Before I answer your question, may I ask you one?

When you think of Matt, or any other loved one who has died, how do you imagine them in relation to yourself? Do you believe they see you? Do you think they can read your mind? Can they feel your grief or share your joy? Are you still somehow connected?

Wondering,
Raffi

DEAREST RAFFI,

I'm glad to hear you came clean. You have restored both my reputation and yours. I'm also glad Eva laughed. I wonder if Franny did.

You are always full of surprises. I'm not sure where all your questions are coming from, but here goes.

Once again, that word "permeable" comes to mind. I think I can absorb the essence of those I have lost, and they mine. We sort-of meld together while remaining separate individuals. The only difference is that from their vantage point they know how to do it better. We don't get the full scope of that type of union in this life. They do. Perhaps not always right away, but eventually. So, I believe the answer to your questions is yes. They can know what I think and how I feel. They can know everything about me. What I don't know is whether they can effect change, alter the course of events. They may be limited to being loving observers.

Everyone I have ever loved and lost is always with me. I have never seen them (as ghosts or phantoms), but I feel them all the time. The main benefit I find for myself is that I am never alone.

What does all of this have to do with my question to you?

Puzzled,
Rachi

DEAR RACHI,

I expected your answer to be something along those lines, and the point I want to make is simple. Those persons you have loved and lost are no longer physically present to you. Nonetheless, they remain with you. You can't hear their voices, but you still carry-on daily conversations with them. It's as if you can hear their voices in your head, guiding you.

That is what you have always done for me. Even before all the letters, during those long stretches of zero contact, there were times your voice played like background music in my head. The words I could make out were based on memories of who you were long ago. Who *you* were to me *then* centered me. Who *I* was to you *then* was my best self. In my head, then as now, the question remains, "What would Rachi think?" I've asked that question a hundred times. The recent variation has become, "What will you think when we meet in October?"

Raffi

DEAR RAFFI,

I loved you then.

I love you now.

I loved you during all the quiet years while our lives were happening.

And I will still love you in October.

You are right. It is simple.

Rachi

Email

MY DEAREST FRIEND,

Thank you.

Raffi

DEAR RAFFI,

Over the last several weeks, I have done a lot of thinking. My primary occupation has become introspection, reevaluation, analysis of my life. I have found a few regrets. Actually, there are more than just a few. If truth be told, there are plenty, but that's not where I'm going with this. Fixating on the low points of my life is not the way I wish to spend all this newfound time I have on my hands.

I am a slight bit surprised to find that, instead, I can begin each day from a place of contentment. Getting here has taken a while and has not been easy. Yet, here I am. I am comfortable in my surroundings, at peace with my family, happy with myself. Dull. Boring. No drama.

Then I feel a little tap on my shoulder. I look up and see you. You are the twinkle in the eye, the flutter in the stomach, the downward plunge of the roller coaster. You are the fun! That is exactly what good friends are for. Matt would agree because I know you offered that fun for him too—as college students and later. It's what brought us together when we were younger. It's what kept Matt and me together all those years. It's what gave all three of us such a connection.

Contentment is fine for every day, but once in a while, we all need *fun*. You're it. Fun is the part that keeps us from getting old.

I can't wait to see you. Summer is almost done.

Love,
Rachi

DEAR RACHI,

Fun, huh? I don't think I've ever been anyone's plaything before. Should I be flattered?

I think I understand what you mean. Everything has been so boring during this pandemic that we are all searching for some lighthearted, enjoyable excitement. I have been grateful to have this trip to look forward to. I was worried for a while that we would need to postpone, but all looks bright right now.

In the meantime, I have done a few consulting jobs for restaurants that are reopening and are in need of updating or revamping. Money is still tight for them, and I am doing what I can to help get things off the ground. So many of these businesses are family operations that have been hurt badly. I've known some of them for years. I must do whatever I can to help. They are doing the same for me in their own way. I know I'm a softy, but if not now, when?

Love,
Raffi

DEAR RACHI,

It's been days since your last email. I hope this means you're busy and not that something is amiss.

Three weeks 'til our departure. I can't wait.

Raffi

Dear Raffi,

I recently discovered something that has stunned me. It took my breath away and I cannot speak about it yet. I need some time.

Rachi

DEAR RACHI,

It sounds serious. Please take all the time you need. I'll be here when you're ready.

Raffi

Dear Rachi,

I'm starting to worry. You don't have to explain if you can't. Just let me know you're all right.

Raffi

Email

DEAR RAFFI,

I am most definitely not all right. Here's the reason.

I was searching for my passport the other day within a box of files containing all of our "important" documents, both Matt's and mine.

Underneath the hanging files, I found an envelope I hadn't noticed before. As it was concealed at the bottom of the box underneath the hanging folders, I had not previously seen it. It contained some letters and cards of a more personal nature, birthday cards and thank-you notes, correspondence that Matt had received throughout the years. To my surprise, I also found a letter referencing an affair, one that Matt had confessed to me more than twenty years ago. I was sadly reminded of the effort on both our parts to win one of the more serious marital battles of our years together.

My shock, therefore, was not about the affair itself, but rather finding that this letter was from you. Matt did not keep his secret from me, but you kept secret the fact that you knew.

The date on your letter struck me, and I remembered the picture of you we discussed some time ago. Sure enough, the letter was dated the very same day you had come to Chicago for the opening. In the photo, you were standing in front of the new restaurant bar, a big smile on your glowing face. As I took a closer look at the photo, I spotted a reflection in that mirror. The quality was too grainy to recognize the face, but this time I had no problem recognizing the pattern on the winter scarf around Matt's neck. That pattern must have registered somehow in my psyche, rendering the picture familiar.

You have known all along. It's no wonder you never answered my questions about that night.

Rachi

Email

Dear Rachi,

I hardly know where to begin. We are going back over twenty years.

Let me start by saying that I see myself in many roles. Playing the "protector" is not one of them. Yet, I am happy to assume that part when it comes to Eva, Samuel, and of course, you.

Let me also say that I don't fall into deep friendship easily with other men. I have never been "just one of the guys." But I had a strong bond with Matthew, as evidenced by the fact that he shared with me one of the most difficult times of his life.

That same time, in retrospect, was not one of my finest moments as I managed to fail both him as a friend and you as a protector.

I never knew about the affair while it was going on. Matt only shared it with me when it was over, and he was conflicted as to whether or not to tell you. He realized the possibly disastrous outcome of confessing and, surprisingly, sought my advice.

If you found the letter I sent, you already know that that night in the restaurant I tried to stop him. Sure, I could have *called* him later to follow up, but I thought if I put all the pros and cons down on paper, he would see things more clearly and come to the same conclusion: not to confess his affair to you.

I'm sorry if finding out that I have known all this time is painful for you. How could I have revealed that fact without causing further pain? I knew the two of you had worked through it. My knowledge of the situation changed nothing. Please let me know you understand.

Raffi

Email

DEAR RAFFI,

We are not going back twenty years. We are going back mere months. We went back and forth in our letters about the ups and downs of that night in the photo. It never occurred to you to bring up something so important? What makes you think I still need protecting now, or even that I needed it back then when it had happened? How did you come to the conclusion that the way to protect me is to keep things from me?

That's what you believed then. That's what you told Matt to do. That's what you're still doing now. Do you really believe "ignorance is bliss"?

R

DEAREST RACHI,

Do you really believe "the truth will set you free"? I was so angry at Matt that a part of me hoped you would set *him* free.

I know how this sounds coming from me, but I was angry at Matt for cheating. I could not accept the fact that anyone could be that careless with your trust, a trust I valued then and still cherish to this day. Once I got past the anger, I was relieved to know that they had at least been discreet enough for no one else to find out, and that you would not face any social embarrassment, so to speak, or discomfort when you were within your circle of friends. Another sigh of relief came from finding out that she was not someone you knew.

I couldn't help thinking that the telling was being done more for himself, to clear his conscience, than out of any consideration for you.

I called him a coward for not being strong enough to carry his secret. I told him to go to Confession and "to sin no more." I saw no way he could tell you without hurting you. No matter what you decided afterward, the pain would always be there.

Was I so wrong in wanting to spare you both from that? In a way, I wasn't only trying to protect you, but Matt as well. This was not about a one-night stand in a strange city after one drink too many. It was an affair, an emotional involvement that had continued for a while. That fact alone was bound to make things much more painful for you. But watching you struck by pain that he had caused would hit Matt just as hard. After all, whatever else he may have doubted during that brief period of estrangement, his love for you was never in question.

As far as the photo goes, how could I have said anything about meeting Matt that night without risking having to explain why we hadn't wanted you to know?

Raffi

RAFFI,

I need more time.

R

DEAR RAFFI,

Once again, I've been feeling a sense of loss. And not only loss but also confusion, turmoil. For a brief moment, I started to rethink our trip.

Neither one of us has been completely honest. I, out of hurt and embarrassment, a need for privacy. You, out of loyalty to Matt, a desire to protect me.

Who I am to you has not changed with this great revelation because you knew everything all along. But your knowing all along changes who you are to me. It inserts an intimacy between us that I wasn't prepared for. It makes my sense of humiliation more public now that I know you were in the audience. Sharing things that are deep and hidden about ourselves with each other should be a conscious choice by each of us. In psychology we know that everyone has secrets. Revealing them is usually a big deal, a major breakthrough. I just found out that my secret had, without my knowledge, already been shared. Of course, I was aware that the other woman knew, but she didn't count. You do.

I vacillate between being hurt and strangely relieved.

A storm.
A calm.
Another storm.

That's what's been happening inside me over the last few days.
I keep re-reading that old letter to Matt followed by some of your more recent ones to me.

You were right. Nothing was ever the same again.

Have you ever broken a bone? I fractured my foot once. There was never a complete break or surgery or a cast, but I limped for quite a while and am reminded of the fracture every time the weather changes.

That's what happened with Matt. I limped for a while, unsteady, not sure exactly how to act or how I was supposed to feel. Afterward, if I noticed the slightest change in him or in our relationship, I remembered the fracture.

Not telling me might have spared me that. Is that what you were trying to do?

In the end, Matt made the decision based on his need at the time. A part of me wonders if he was hoping I would not forgive. My response would determine both our fates. Did he leave the choice to me out of cowardice or out of love?

All I know for sure is that despite that fracture as well as others along the way, for Matt and me, it was not only the marriage that survived, but our love. That may not have been the case if anyone else had entered the narrative and my humiliation had been more public at the time. Any other person entering the equation, even if that person was my best friend, might have tipped the scale in another direction.

Looking back, with the wisdom of hindsight, perhaps both Matt and you made the right decision, he to share and you to withhold. The marriage survived. And, as far as I'm concerned, our friendship did, as well. If you recall, not so long ago I said I would still love you in October.

Still here,
Rachi

Email

Dear Rachi,

If a whirlwind hits Chicago, it is only me breathing a great sigh of relief. I am happy to read that our friendship remains intact.

And just to set the record straight, my friendship with Matt was no worse for the wear. Lord knows I gave him plenty of occasions to be angry with my choices, as well.

I am sorry that finding my letter brought you such turmoil. I can't help wondering why Matt kept it, especially since he decided against my advice. I do understand your instinct to keep this entire episode private, between you and Matt. Rereading your letter, I see why my knowing all along might be upsetting, especially if you think it influences how I see you. I never, however, regarded Matt's actions as a reflection on you. The way you chose to handle his indiscretion, in my opinion, made you more admirable, strong not weak. Since we are finally discussing the incident now, I can tell you that Matt was never the same again, either. He was forever grateful that neither of you had walked away from what was most important in his life. I'm not sure he ever forgave himself.

As for myself, I am truly sorry if I failed as your knight in shining armor. I promise never to fail as your friend.

Glad you're back,
Raffi

DEAR RAFFI,

Thank you for understanding my need to work through this. I think it is rooted in my family upbringing and the rule of not airing our dirty laundry outside of our own household. I believe the same was true for you in regards to your mother's illness. We were always fearful of someone finding out that we were less than perfect. In my case, you probably already know that, but even so, I guess I am embarrassed. So many years later, the feeling of not being enough is compounded by the fact that someone else knows that I wasn't. If I had known it then, my decision would have been that much harder. It also would have been the same.

Anyway, my reaction has more to do with how I feel about me than how I feel about you.

I still love you.

By the way, I did find my passport.

I am no longer conflicted about our trip, but I will ask for one small favor. Let's agree to leave this topic for another time. It should not join us on our trip. It may need more discussion, but not now, not then.

Somewhat subdued,
Rachi

Dear Rachi,

Happy to hear that you continue to want me as your travel companion and that you are ready to go.

Please don't assume that what happened back then diminished you in any way. What Matt did was his fault, not yours. And as far as I am concerned, your decision, as I said before, showed courage and compassion, strength not weakness. You have nothing to feel embarrassed about. I am only sorry it took twenty years to tell you that. I could have waited to tell you when we meet, but you know me, I think it's important to put it in writing. I am also happy not to discuss it any further until the far distant future.

About our trip, I have a wish.

It's more so an expectation: may our dinners in Portugal and Italy be as vivid and warm—and painted in all the colors of joy—as your Christmas Eve dinners during our college years.

Speaking of important things, my door is finally ready for your inspection, and hopefully, your approval and appreciation. You are among the select few that will immediately "get it."

The evening I went through the paint colors with the painter, I invited him in for one or two of my famous Manhattans. He turned out to be a rather colorful man, no pun intended, and we made an evening of it. I thought there was something amiss when I didn't see him for a couple of days. Then, one evening I returned home from a visit with Eva and found the job completed—but not with the color I had chosen. It took me only a few moments to realize his choice was not only better than mine, but perfect.

I can't wait for you to see it.

One more week until the big reveal of who we are to each other. Are you packed and ready?

Love,
Raffi

DEAR RAFFI,

Yes, I am ready. And I fully expect our dinners in Europe to provide us with the same comforting memories ten years from now that our dinners fifty years ago provide us with today.

Although, as epic as our dinners will be, the real comfort will come from our feasting on the words of fifty years, our back-and-forth correspondence, our timid revelations, our confessions, our humor, our pain, letters that stripped away boundaries and allowed us to share. Still, I have a feeling that there is so much more to know.

Tomorrow we will at long last meet face to face. I'm starting to get butterflies, again.

Is there anything I should know about this new, artistic entrance?

What color is your door, dammit?

Love,
Rachi

DEAR RACHI,

Our next correspondence will be by text when you arrive here tomorrow.

The guest room is ready with fresh linens, fresh toiletries, and fresh flowers. (I have no idea what my cleaning woman is thinking.) You may recall that my bedrooms are adorned with prints from Gustav Klimt, one of my favorite artists. You will have the *Apple Tree I* room. It is not the same tree as that of Adam and Eve in the Garden of Eden. As a matter of fact, no one knows for sure what the subject matter may have symbolized for the artist. However, it is generally referred to as an "optimistic" piece, thereby making it the perfect choice for our re-encounter and for your brief stay.

I am also preordering dinner and will have fresh brioche for our coffee in the morning.

I can't believe I have butterflies, too.

I want the door to be a surprise, dammit.

See you soon.

Love,
Raffi

RACHI: Oh my! The elevator doors have opened and I am confronted by the brightest, reddest color I have ever seen. Am I gazing at a maraschino cherry? It's all about the Manhattans, isn't it? Is there one of those waiting for me on the other side? Do I need to knock?

RAFFI: There is no need to knock. For you, my bright red door always remains unlocked. Please walk right in. I am waiting inside, a smile on my face, a drink in each hand, my complement to the feast of words that is about to begin.

ACKNOWLEDGEMENTS

I humbly thank the family and friends that always believe in me; the artist behind my cover who offers no resistance to conducting our meetings over lunch; my parents that always gave me a voice; and my editor who helps to place that voice on a written page.

FOR MORE ON MARIA GIUSEPPA, VISIT US AT
WWW.CHRISTOPHERWHISPERINGS.COM
BOOK GROUP QUESTIONS AND IDEAS AVAILABLE AT
WWW.CHRISTOPHERWHISPERINGS.COM
TEACHER RESOURCES AND CLASSROOM DISCUSSION PROMPTS AVAILABLE AT
WWW.CHRISTOPHERWHISPERINGS.COM